"Thanks for going along with her scheme," Jack said.

"Scheme?" Cassie questioned.

"Yes, my mother is trying to find me the perfect wife."

"And will you be the perfect husband?"

To Jack, there was no mistaking the scorn in her melodious voice. "I have no idea if I will or not," he said. "I've never been a husband. Care to help me practice?" Now why had he said *that*? Just because she was nice to look at didn't mean he wanted to get involved with someone who made her living selling bugs.

Cassie's cheeks grew pink. "Of course I don't want to help you practice! What kind of woman do you think I am?"

"Not any kind I've ever met before."

Dear Reader:

The spirit of the Silhouette Romance Homecoming Celebration lives on as each month we bring you six books by continuing stars!

And we have a galaxy of stars planned for 1988. In the coming months, we're publishing romances by many of your favorite authors such as Annette Broadrick, Sondra Stanford and Brittany Young. And that's not all—during the summer, Diana Palmer presents her most engaging heroes and heroines in a trilogy that will be sure to capture your heart!

Your response to these authors and other authors of Silhouette Romances has served as a touchstone for us, and we're pleased to bring you more books with Silhouette's distinctive medley of charm, wit and—above all—romance.

I hope you enjoy this book and the many stories to come. Come home to romance—for always!

Sincerely,

Tara Hughes
Senior Editor
Silhouette Books

PAMELA TOTH

The Ladybug Lady

Silhouette Romance

Published by Silhouette Books New York

America's Publisher of Contemporary Romance

This one's for Erika and for Melody,
beautiful and special daughters who fill me
with pride and joy and love.

SILHOUETTE BOOKS
300 E. 42nd St., New York, N.Y. 10017

ISBN: 0-373-08595-8

First Silhouette Books printing August 1988

Books by Pamela Toth

Silhouette Romance

Kissing Games #500
The Ladybug Lady #595

Silhouette Special Edition

Thunderstruck #411

PAMELA TOTH

was born in Wisconsin but now makes her home near Seattle, Washington, with her husband and two daughters. She enjoys bowling, roller-skating, and camping with her family, but for the last four years has devoted much time to writing romances. Pamela says she gets many of her ideas simply from reading the newspaper, when various occupations and stories trigger her imagination to create original scenes and characters.

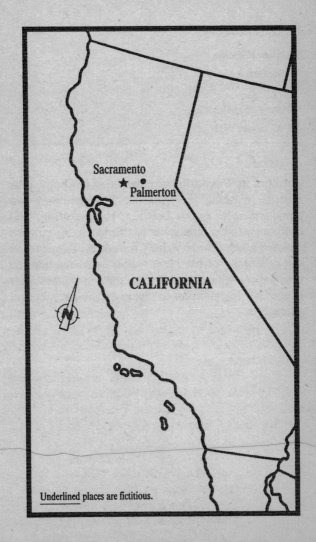

Sacramento

Palmerton

CALIFORNIA

Underlined places are fictitious.

Chapter One

Pausing to pull on worn garden gloves, Cassie Culpepper squatted beside a row of pea vines before glancing toward the empty, silent backyard next door. For a moment her gaze rested on the red-and-yellow swing set and the neatly tended flower garden. Cassie realized with a sigh how much she would miss the Petersons, her former neighbors, who had recently moved to Washington State with their three children.

She hoped the new people would be as nice and as easy to get along with, and that they would share her views on chemical-free gardening as the Petersons had. Cassie hated the idea of anyone using pesticides near her vegetables.

As she leaned over to investigate an early sign of infestation on a curling pea vine, a deafening roar split the quiet of the late morning. At first Cassie thought the sound came from a lawn mower or a chain saw. Then suddenly, with a sharp squawk of protest, she leaped to her feet, realizing what the loud, throbbing racket might be. The trowel fell from her fingers, and she broke into a run.

Pausing only long enough to unlatch the gate, she raced to the front yard. Seconds later she skidded to a stop, her worst fears confirmed. Already clouds of toxic moisture were drifting toward her property and her organic vegetables on the faint breeze that stirred the warm air.

A man was *spraying* the bushes next door!

The culprit stood with his back toward Cassie, hose in hand. His white tanker truck was parked on the shoulder of the road, its loud pump forcing noxious chemicals through the hose and into the air. Her air!

"Stop that right now!" Cassie hollered angrily. Fear for her vegetables and for the thousands of ladybugs she had released the day before added strength to her usually mellow voice, but the man gave no indication that he'd heard.

Cassie stepped forward, intending to cross the forty feet or so that separated them and again order him to stop. Then she hesitated, having no desire to venture closer to the rapidly spreading cloud of choking vapors. Even the operator wore some kind of protective covering over his head.

For a moment Cassie stood and indecisively nibbled her full lower lip. Normally a nonviolent person, she felt a blinding urge to beat up the man who was polluting her environment. She could see that he was big, with heavily muscled shoulders and arms under the damp, faded blue shirt that strained across his back. Equally faded jeans molded slim hips and long legs. Cassie realized right away that physical violence was definitely a dumb idea.

The pump throbbed on and the misty spray belched from the hose he held as Cassie stamped her foot with frustration. She shouted again, reluctant to get any closer. Nearly frantic now to stop the flow, she clenched her fists. In sheer desperation, she finally took several steps toward the man and her foot hooked on something, nearly sending her sprawling. Flushing hotly, she recovered her balance and glanced down.

The garden hose!

The cloud was drifting closer to her defenseless garden, and Cassie's only thought was to stop the outpouring of poison. She lunged toward the outside faucet, giving it several quick turns. Racing forward again, she gripped the nozzle, aiming it toward the middle of the man's sweat-soaked back, and squeezed the trigger.

Several things happened almost simultaneously. The stream of silvery water hit dead on target, the pump's deafening racket clacked to a halt and the man's deep bellow of enraged surprise roared through the sudden silence.

Cassie's nerveless fingers released the nozzle handle, cutting off the flow of water as the man whirled toward her, tearing off his face shield. For someone so big, his movements were surprisingly quick. The overwhelming audacity of what she had just done hit her at the same instant as the icy blast from his cold blue eyes.

It took his long legs mere seconds to cover the ground between them, and Cassie had to force herself not to shrink from the anger that radiated toward her in waves. If anything, she had underestimated his physical power.

"Why the hell did you do that?" he shouted.

"I, uh . . ."

"What?" he shouted again, obviously frustrated.

"I wanted to stop you," she said, her voice gaining strength as some of her anger returned.

"*What?*" Then a disgusted look crossed the broad, tanned face as the man yanked off one work glove. Cassie watched, puzzled, as he poked a finger in his ear. Pulling out a small yellow object, he did the same to the other side.

Earplugs!

For a moment he looked sheepish, then he glowered down at her again.

Jack had no more idea why the woman who stood before him, cheeks stained an angry red and brown eyes snapping with temper, was upset than he did why she'd turned the water on him. He knew he didn't have the wrong address. Anyway, the hose at her feet stretched to the house next door. As he stared down at her, puzzlement and irritation warring within him, the wet fabric of his shirt became uncomfortable against his skin. Without thinking he flicked open the buttons and peeled off the worn garment.

The woman's eyes widened, and she took a step backward, her thoughts as easy to read as the Sunday funnies. Grinning reluctantly at her comical expression, Jack used the wet shirt to mop at the trickle of perspiration running down the side of his neck, his eyes never leaving hers.

"Why did you do that?" he asked once more, his tone calmer as he studied her closely and waited for an explanation.

Long, curling dark hair was pulled back from an oval face and spilled over her shoulders. Big brown eyes narrowed as she returned his stare. Damn, she was cute, but obviously unbalanced, and she still hadn't answered his question.

Cassie's temper boiled dangerously when she saw the smug grin pull at the corners of the man's mouth. He'd seen the way her eyes widened when he removed the wet shirt from his deeply tanned torso. For one confused moment she didn't know what he had in mind, then her eyes were drawn to his furry chest and her mouth went dry. She felt her anger begin to dissolve like the grease stain on a detergent commercial. Sharply she yanked her wandering attention back to the man's transgression.

She forced her gaze to remain on his arrogant face, but that didn't do much for her momentary befuddlement. He was a singularly attractive man, and probably well aware of it. His hair, even mussed and sweat darkened, was streaked with a hundred varying shades of bronze and blond. Thick eyebrows and dark lashes framed his intense blue eyes, and a bushy mustache bracketed an expressive mouth. Cassie shivered with reaction.

"I'm still waiting," he said in a dry voice.

His comment reminded Cassie why she was there on her front lawn facing a stranger she'd just attempted to drown with a plastic hose. Bubbling indignation returned in a heady rush.

"What do you think *you* were doing?" she asked, her voice rising with every word.

One thick, blond eyebrow quirked. "Seems to me I was doing my job," he retorted. "What'd it look like to you?"

Cassie's color deepened. "You're spreading poison," she almost squeaked. "Those chemicals are deadly."

His expression hardened and his brows pulled together into a frown. "Now wait just a damn minute. I don't use anything harmful to humans or to animals."

Fighting a feeling of intimidation, Cassie jammed her fists onto her hips and thrust out her jaw. She took a deep breath, and her Save the Whales T-shirt strained across her feminine curves.

"Oh, yeah? What about harmful to insects, or don't they count?" she demanded.

The man opened his mouth, then shut it again as bafflement filled his face. "That's the whole reason I'm spraying," he said in confusion.

"Aha!" Cassie gloated in satisfaction. "You're exactly right."

Jack scratched his head, feeling as though he was chasing himself in circles. It was a damn shame that a girl as cute as the one standing in front of him apparently had an elevator that didn't go all the way to her top floor. He appreciated women who were good-looking, but found them boring as hell if they didn't have at least average intelligence, too.

"Somewhere you've lost me," he admitted.

"You're killing insects," she repeated, waving her arms. "The good with the bad. It's indiscriminate homicide!"

"I'm only spraying for web caterpillars. If they've made one positive contribution to humanity, no one has told me about it." Jack felt as if he was trying to explain himself to a weirdo and couldn't resist a hint of sarcasm. All that junk she was spouting about good insects made no sense.

Cassie shook her head, exasperated. "You're polluting my air, contaminating my garden and killing the ladybugs I put out yesterday! And I want you to stop right this minute!" She shook a finger at him, and the tone of her voice made it perfectly clear that she thought he was being irresponsible.

"You're spreading bugs?" he asked, looking more confused than ever.

"Ladybugs," she corrected him. "I sell them, by mail order."

"Of course," he muttered. Then he ran a hand through his streaked hair, making it stand up in untidy spikes. "Are you some kind of a nut, or just a flaming environmentalist kook?" he asked, staring pointedly at the logo on her shirt.

Cassie flushed at his words, then made a determined effort to hang on to her temper. "Ladybugs eat garden pests," she explained, trying to be patient. "People who raise organic vegetables use them for control instead of sprays. Sprays which, by the way, can kill us and turn our unborn children into mutants!"

The man rolled his eyes. "Are you pregnant?" he asked, looking at her flat stomach with interest.

Cassie flushed and shook her head.

"My sprays wouldn't hurt you if you were," he continued with vehemence. "I'm *very careful*."

"Oh, how so?" She tapped one bare foot impatiently, calling his attention to her long legs. For a moment he was distracted, then hastily he collected his scattering thoughts.

"I always caution my customers to keep their animals inside until the spray has dried." He groped further, trying mightily to keep his gaze from her smooth thighs and shapely calves and to remember more of the instructional pamphlet he'd read that morning. Operating one of the trucks for a business he hadn't even wanted wasn't how he'd planned to spend his day, but the owner of a piece of property he needed wouldn't sell unless Sierra Pest Control was part of the package. Then one driver had quit abruptly, and he found himself with a fistful of orders and no one to fill them. And he was now responsible for two employees who needed their jobs.

"I use legal chemicals, tested and approved by the United States government," he added. "In fact, we just began using Raydelon II, the newest and safest pesticide on the market."

Cassie snorted with disgust at the triumphant expression on his face. "And you wear a protective shield," she added.

"That's right," he agreed.

"See!" she exclaimed, jabbing a finger at him again, her full lips breaking into a victorious grin.

The man frowned as Cassie shoved her point home.

"Your chemicals *are* harmful, or you wouldn't have to wear a shield and warn the neighbors about their pets," she concluded. "*That's* why I turned the water on you!" Without giving the man a chance to reply, she bestowed a self-satisfied nod and turned away, dragging the long, green hose behind her. After several steps she glanced over her shoulder. He was still standing there, looking slightly bemused as if he was trying to pick his way through her reasoning.

"And, if you start that thing again," she threatened, pointing to the obviously expensive, newly painted rig, as if it were a garbage truck, "I'll do it again."

Jack watched her in silence, a wide grin stretching the corners of his mouth, as she turned and retreated, taking the hose with her. Despite her strange ideas about bugs, she had a way of walking that shifted her hips enticingly in the brief turquoise shorts. He could certainly relate to that, even if he hadn't made much sense of her argument.

Checking his watch, he picked up the soggy shirt and the mask he'd dropped earlier, then began loading his equipment into the spotless truck. He was due at another appointment, so he'd have to finish this job later, after he'd straightened out the problem with the loony neighbor. All in all, it had been a rather unusual morning.

Cassie was still seething about the incident the next day, muttering to her cucumber plants under her breath. She would just have to talk to the new neighbors as soon as possible and hope they'd understand about not spraying their yard. It was too dangerous! She decided to run next door and introduce herself after she'd weeded another row and washed up.

"Darn!" she exclaimed through clenched teeth. The cutworms had beaten her to it. Five of the newly sprouted vines lay on the rich dirt, their green leaves already wilting in the warm morning air. They'd been neatly snipped off at ground level.

Cassie groaned. It looked as if her bad luck was holding. Then, as she carefully probed the soil around the decapitated plants, a friendly greeting drew her attention toward the backyard next door.

A silver-haired woman wearing a pastel print housedress was leaning on the fence that separated the two properties. "Hi," she said as Cassie rose and walked closer. "I'm Mattie Hoffman."

Cassie pulled off her soiled gloves before she introduced herself. "I'm glad to meet you." That solved one of her problems; now to find a way to bring up yesterday's disaster.

"My husband, Fred, and I just moved in last week," Mrs. Hoffman continued. "This is such a nice, quiet neighborhood, isn't it?"

"Umm, yes," Cassie agreed. "It sure is." Most of the time, she added silently, recalling her shouting match the morning before.

"Do you have children?" The older woman's smile was open and friendly as she eyed the tire swing hanging from an aging apple tree next to Cassie's large garden.

"No," Cassie replied. "I'm not married."

The smile widened, the woman's blue eyes twinkling through the lenses of her wire-framed glasses. She looked Cassie up and down swiftly, glancing at her lavender halter top and purple striped running shorts.

"I wonder..." Mattie said, positively beaming. "Would you be free to come over to a barbecue this evening?" At Cassie's look of surprise, she continued quickly. "Nothing fancy, just my daughter and her family, and my son. It would be a chance to get acquainted."

Cassie thought for a moment. Perhaps there would be an opportunity to discuss the matter so crucial to her. It was certainly worth a try.

"I'd love to, but you must let me bring something. A salad?"

Mattie nodded. "If you'd like, that would be very nice," she said, lingering for a few more moments before excusing herself.

When five o'clock rolled around, Cassie was ready. She had made a pasta salad from curly noodles and some of the things out of her garden, and marinated the mixture in her own homemade Italian dressing. Next to gardening, cooking was one of her favorite activities.

Dark hair still damp from a recent shower curled softly around her face and hung loosely down her back. She'd touched her lips with tinted gloss, darkened her eyelids with frosted brown shadow that she normally only bothered with for very special occasions and added a dab of perfume to her throat. She had even donned a sundress of blue-and-green stripes in honor of the occasion and was feeling ready for just about anything.

After Cassie had rung her neighbor's bell, she was greeted by Mattie, who took the salad dish and led her into the backyard. There on a redwood deck, Cassie met Mattie's husband, Fred Hoffman, a balding man with a large build and gray mustache.

Next, Mattie introduced Cassie to their daughter and her family. Karen was petite like her mother and had blond hair. Her husband, Ben, was tall with dark hair and glasses, and their two little boys both had big brown eyes. The younger one hid behind his father, but the older one, who looked about seven, boldly walked up to Cassie.

Staring intently, he said, "I'm Lance. Are you going to marry my uncle?"

Karen groaned as Cassie's mouth dropped open. "I'm afraid not," Cassie answered, recovering quickly as Lance's smile drooped. "I don't even know your uncle."

Both Ben and Karen began to speak at the same time, apologizing for their son's outspoken question.

Cassie smiled and made a deprecating gesture with one hand. "Don't worry about it," she said, winking at the boy, who began to grin again.

Karen glanced at her watch and then turned toward her mother. "Where is . . ."

"Oh, I hear a car door!" Mattie exclaimed. "Now you'll get to meet our son," she told Cassie.

A sudden light of warning blinked on in Cassie's brain. Mattie had glossed over things so quickly that morning, but now it occurred to Cassie that the other woman might have invited her over for a specific reason and not just to be neighborly! It wouldn't be the first time Cassie had been offered to someone's unmarried son like some kind of human sacrifice.

Usually it was Cassie's own mother and her friends who were responsible for the awkward pairings. Blind dates and surprise dinner guests were their specialties. Cassie's mother couldn't seem to understand why Cassie wasn't eager to meet some nice young man and settle down. She meddled in Cassie's brother's life with equal enthusiasm and, so far, equal lack of success. Like Cassie, Tom had given up putting a stop to Mrs. Culpepper's matchmaking, instead merely scuttling her plans whenever possible, enduring or avoiding them the rest of the time.

"Come in, dear," Mattie called. "We're all on the back deck. I want you to meet someone. I just know you'll like her."

"Mom..." There was reproach in the deep voice.

Cassie watched the doorway with curiosity, hoping fervently that the older woman never had the opportunity to join forces with her own mother. Mattie came through, talking over her shoulder the whole time.

"Cassie, dear," she said, turning, "I want you to meet our son. Jack, this is our sweet new neighbor, Miss Cassie Culpepper."

Even as Cassie stood and faced the man she instantly recognized as her adversary of the morning before, the thought crossed her mind that her bad luck was holding. Cassie lumped a second meeting with the jerk she now knew as Jack Hoffman in the same category as finding cutworms on her cucumbers, and it took real willpower to keep her bland smile from fading.

The heavily fringed blue eyes staring down at her widened in surprise, then narrowed thoughtfully as what looked like an innocent grin spread beneath the full mustache.

"Pleased to meet you." His deep voice rumbled up from the broad chest that Cassie remembered was deeply tanned and dusted with blond hair. This evening it was modestly covered with a neatly pressed light blue shirt tucked into navy shorts.

Once again she was made achingly aware of the man's magnetic looks. The pale color of the shirt was the perfect foil for his blond hair and dark skin, and it intensified the deeper shade of his eyes. Since he was acting as if he'd never seen her before, she decided to go along with the deception, at least temporarily. She placed her hand into his much larger one, pulling it back out of his warm grip almost immediately.

"Nice to meet you, too," she managed, her voice sounding strained even to her own ears. Realizing that her gaze had settled on his brown throat, she forced herself to look back into his face as Mattie clucked happily around both of them.

Jack Hoffman's eyes were as sexy as Cassie remembered, and they bore traces of the humor she had glimpsed the day before. The smile on his full mouth dented a dimple into one lean cheek. As she gazed up at him, Cassie absently wiggled fingers that still tingled from the warmth of his handclasp.

Jack tore his attention away to greet his sister and her husband, but before he could utter a word, two blurs of motion attached themselves to his bare legs.

"Uncle Jack, Uncle Jack! Will you play catch with us?"

As he started to answer his nephews, Mattie cut in.

"I need you two to help me carry out the food. Let Uncle Jack talk to Cassie for a while."

Jack groaned silently. His mother's intentions were as clear as her newly polished windows. She bemoaned the fact that he hadn't seen fit to settle down and provide her with more grandchildren.

Usually he played along with her harmless meddling, but now it was time to draw the line, and he'd just have to speak to her the first chance he got. Still, her taste was improving, he conceded as he shot a glance at Cassie. The dress she had on was even more flattering than her brief shorts had been.

After giving him a broad wink, Karen followed Mattie and the children into the house. Jack glanced around but Ben and Fred had moved to the brick barbecue at the other end of the deck and were talking animatedly.

Turning to Cassie, Jack realized once again how pretty she was. Her big dark eyes were regarding him with something less than enthusiasm and, since no one else was within earshot, he spoke quickly. "Thanks for going along with the deception. Mom has high blood pressure, and I like to let her think I'm cooperating with her little schemes."

"Schemes?" Cassie's voice was questioning. She knew perfectly well what he meant, but the complacency of his tone needed puncturing. Let him spell it out.

"She's trying to find me the perfect wife."

"And will you be the perfect husband?"

To Jack there was no mistaking the scorn in her melodious voice. The kitten had claws. How could he have forgotten that important fact?

"I have no idea if I will or not," he said. "I've never been a husband. Care to help me practice?" Now why had he said *that*? Just because she was nice to look at, with a slim but curvaceous figure that went very nicely with her pretty face, didn't mean he wanted to get involved with someone who made her living selling bugs.

Cassie's cheeks grew pink. "Of course I don't want to help you practice!" she snapped. "What kind of woman do you think I am?"

"Not any kind I've ever met before," he said with a smug grin.

The man was certainly conceited, and his mother's matchmaking schemes had undoubtedly added to his inflated opinion of himself. He'd probably had women falling all over him since he'd been in the sandbox. The image brought a reluctant twitch to Cassie's lips as she pictured a much younger version of herself dumping a bucket of the stuff over his blond head.

Before either of them could say anything further, Lance and his younger brother, Andy, who was five, slid open the screen door and began bringing out bowls of food. Cassie stepped away from Jack quickly.

He noticed her action and grinned. "Retreating?" he questioned under his breath.

"Not on your life!" Cassie shot back before she realized how her answer would sound.

"Glad to hear it," he murmured before he turned to relieve Lance of a deviled egg platter that had tipped alarmingly.

A little while later, after eating more than she would have thought possible, Cassie leaned back in the lawn chair and sighed. She liked all of Mattie's family, with only one exception.

If she and Jack had met differently, she was pretty sure she would have liked him, too, despite the fact that he had more self-assurance than any one man was entitled to. The way his eyes twinkled when he said something outrageous, she was never sure if he was conceited or self-mocking.

There had been no opportunity to bring up the spraying, and now that she knew who Jack was, it would be hard to mention it at all. Still, the subject was vital to her own business. Perhaps she could appeal directly to Jack's good side, providing, of course, that he had one.

As Mattie refilled the iced-tea glasses and brought the men more beer, the conversation turned to a discussion of a new restaurant on the outskirts of town. Karen and Ben had eaten there several nights before, and she was telling Jack how good the food was when Mattie touched his arm.

"Why don't you and Cassie try it out?" she asked.

Jack sent his mother a telling look before he glanced at Cassie. Her cheeks were pink, and her soft lips began to form what he knew would be an embarrassed demurral. Before he could stop himself, an imp took control of his tongue.

"Yes, Cassie, let's do that. How about tomorrow evening?"

Cassie's eyes widened. Didn't he know the spot he had put her on? She was sure he had no more desire to take her to dinner than she had to go with him. Still, the big coward had dropped the whole mess in her lap instead of standing up to his mother's too-obvious plotting. And he wasn't aware that Cassie needed to talk to him.

She knew that he expected her to refuse, taking the blame for raising Mattie's blood pressure on herself. Well, the heck with that. If he didn't have the nerve to set his mother straight, he deserved to stew in his own, macho juices!

"What a wonderful idea," she cooed up at him, batting her eyelashes and enjoying the parade of expressions that flashed across his handsome face. "What time will you be picking me up?"

Jack blinked with surprise, her words rendering him temporarily speechless. What game was she playing? He hadn't really considered taking crazy Miss Culpepper out, but there was nothing more he could say with Mattie beaming at the two of them as though she had invented love.

Swallowing, he remembered the sight of Cassie walking away the day before, all long legs and slim but rounded curves. It made him realize that there might be compensations to his mother's meddling. Never one to miss an opportunity, especially when it landed right in his lap, he grinned wolfishly.

"How's seven suit you?"

Somehow his voice didn't sound nearly as disappointed as Cassie thought it should.

"Seven's fine." Even as the words left her mouth, she eyed Jack with suspicion, aware that he was smiling as if he had access to a very private joke. Now what had her sharp tongue and crazy impulses gotten her into? And had she won this round, or lost it?

Chapter Two

Cassie was finally getting used to the startled, often amused glances she got whenever she drove her car. When her brother, Tom, had offered to repair the Volkswagen Bug after a minor fender bender, only charging the cost of the new paint, Cassie should have been suspicious, knowing him and his sometimes offbeat sense of humor. At the time, he'd insisted he was doing it as a favor between siblings, telling her that his reward would come when she recommended him to other potential customers.

After the initial shock wore off, Cassie had begun to enjoy the attention her bright red Beetle with black spots always attracted. The free advertising she got from the words *The Ladybug Lady* printed on the door in black letters was nice, too. Tom had tried to talk her into twin antennas mounted on the front of the car to look like, well, antennae, but Cassie had drawn the line there.

As she grinned at a neatly dressed older man in a dark sedan who almost ran the stop sign when he saw her car, she couldn't help but ponder just how her own conservative father felt about his two offbeat offspring. Dad was a dentist and had planned for both children to complete college and then enter a profession.

At least Tom had finished, but after obtaining a bachelor's degree in graphic art, he'd gone to vocational school and opened a body repair shop. Between fabulous custom paint jobs and referrals from classmates who now sold insurance, Tom was doing quite well. He'd even had a request to do another VW like Cassie's, but refused on the grounds that hers was one of a kind. Instead the owner now drove what looked like a giant green turtle.

Cassie, on the other hand, had only lasted one year before dropping out of the university. Since then she'd held a string of jobs, from school library clerk to department store cashier, while taking all the gardening classes she could. She'd bought her little house and the two acres behind it with her share of an inheritance from her father's sister and finally had the room for an organic garden.

The ladybugs had started out as a sideline, but had quickly developed into a business that promised to eventually pay her day-to-day expenses. That and the weekly gardening column she did that had recently become syndicated, occasional classes and demonstrations were beginning to bring in enough money to keep her independent. If things didn't work out, she could probably go back to the boutique where she'd filled in before. Or something else would come along.

Her father seemed to have adjusted quite well to her life-style, which didn't surprise Cassie. "Find something

that makes you happy,'' he'd always said, but she knew
he still hoped that she'd finish school. In the meantime,
he bragged about her to all his patients and had even sent
her a few customers.

Cassie's mother, though herself an avid gardener, was
slower to offer her full support. There was a considerable gap between hybrid tea roses and organic eggplants,
and Mrs. Culpepper made it very clear she would rather
that Cassie was raising her grandchildren instead of organic vegetables.

Most of the ladybug business was by mail. Even now,
Cassie was driving home from the UPS office. She'd
dropped off a shipment of live insects that she'd spent the
morning packing and addressing. The rest of yesterday's
harvest of *Hippodamia convergens* had been separated
from the twigs and dirt gathered along with them, washed
and put into cold storage. There were approximately
seventy-two thousand beetles per gallon carton in four
old refrigerators that lined what had started out as a
double garage before she'd had it rewired.

As she turned into her driveway, Cassie honked and
waved at one of the neighborhood children. They all
found her car funny, almost as funny as the idea that she
kept bugs in the fridge.

A couple of the older kids worked in her garden, and
one made deliveries of vegetables to the downtown stand
that was glad to get anything she sent. Her produce was
always in demand. Cassie had found that hiring the
neighbors went a long way toward keeping down any
pilfering from her garden, and the parents noticed that
their kids were much more willing to eat vegetables they'd
helped raise. All around, the system worked very well,
even if it didn't leave Cassie much spare time.

After parking the colorful car in her driveway, she unlocked the front door of her little house, pushed it open and took a step backward.

"You two have no manners," she said in a mock-scolding voice to the blue point Siamese cats who pushed into the house ahead of her. Neither glanced up as they raced toward the kitchen to check out their food dishes. Even though Cassie only fed them morning and evening, they seemed forever hopeful that something unexpected and delicious would appear. After a quick check of the empty containers, they both wound their lean gray-blue bodies around her ankles as she tried to walk across the room without falling over them.

Stumbling, Cassie gently pushed them away, then glanced at the yellow, plastic, butterfly clock on the wall above the kitchen table. Should she set something out for supper? She really didn't expect Jack Hoffman to show up. After all, his offer to take her to dinner had been made under duress and was only for his mother's benefit... and to embarrass Cassie. Surely Jack had no more real desire for them to spend the evening together than she did.

Ignoring Crystal's loud meow of protest, she stepped back into the hallway and peered at her reflection in the oval mirror there. Her lightly tanned face was free of makeup, and her hair was pulled into a ponytail, the shorter strands curling riotously around her face. After studying the shine on her straight nose, Cassie hurried into her bedroom.

If Jack did come, did she want him to find her in faded jeans and a shabby sweatshirt with cut-off sleeves? Which would be worse, to dress for a date who never arrived or to be caught looking the way she did now? Perhaps she should at least fix her face and hair. Not to go out with him, of course, but just to let him see what he was missing.

"What do you think?" she asked the other cat, striking an exaggerated pose. He sat on the corner of Cassie's water bed, purring. "Black silk and pearls or clown makeup and the patchwork jumpsuit?"

Blake's blue eyes blinked slowly shut, and he purred louder.

"You're a lot of help," Cassie muttered, before sticking her head into the closet. It wouldn't hurt to put on some nice slacks and an attractive blouse, she decided.

"I'll bet you a Tender Treat Gourmet Dinner he doesn't even show," she said to Blake, who yawned widely and washed one paw, unimpressed with the offer.

By the time the doorbell rang at seven, Cassie had showered, curled her hair and painted her short fingernails in a new, frosted ivory polish. For a moment she'd even considered going to the drugstore for a set of artificial press-on nails, before reason returned.

During the whole time she had kept up a running conversation with the two cats, telling them she had no intention of actually going. She had curled the thicket of lashes that surrounded her brown eyes, spritzed her skin with a delicate floral scent and slipped into a mint-green blouse trimmed with lace, and a matching green skirt. Now as the bell chimed again, she checked her stockings for snags, pulled on high-heeled sandals, wiggled her frosted toes and took a deep breath.

"You should have bet me," she said to Blake as she walked by the bed.

As his finger pushed the buzzer a second time, Jack was still surprised to find himself on Cassie's front porch, dressed to kill in a freshly ironed white shirt, dark slacks and an almost brand-new sport coat. His tie tack was a gold scarab, and he wondered if Cassie would appreciate the humor.

All afternoon he had told himself he'd be damned if he'd go over there that evening so she could make a fool out of him by not being home or by shutting the door in his face. Still, he had gone through all the motions of getting ready, and even discovered that he was whistling tunelessly on the way to her house. Now relief uncurled his tightly clenched fists when he glimpsed Cassie through the lace-curtained window.

She was dressed as if she expected him. In fact, she looked gorgeous as she opened the front door and stared up into his face. When he'd pulled into her driveway in his late-model pickup and spotted the strange-looking little car that was parked there, Jack hadn't been sure what to expect next. A caterpillar costume wouldn't have surprised him after the sight of the polka-dotted Volkswagen. She must take her bug business seriously, but at least she wasn't wearing any of the kinkier costumes from *Alice in Wonderland*.

"Hi," he said heartily, thrusting a single, pink rose at her.

"Thank you," Cassie stammered as her fingers automatically wrapped around the long stem. She was still trying to deal with the fact that he was here, on her step, looking better than any man had a right to look.

Below the neatly combed hair and sweeping mustache, his light tan sport coat clung smoothly to his wide shoulders, presenting yet another side to the man she'd already seen in work clothes and casual attire. Each new image was more compelling. Her lips twitched when she noticed his tie tack, and she wondered if he'd chosen it deliberately.

"Come in," she invited, fervently glad she'd taken such pains with her own appearance. When he stepped past her, she allowed her gaze to slide the length of his dark slacks to the Western boots that covered his big feet. The faint scent of some unknown spice tantalized her nostrils as he turned slowly to face her.

"I like this," he said, indicating the small, neat living room. "It's cozy."

Cassie turned to see if he was merely being polite, but there was genuine approval in his blue eyes.

"Thanks," she said again.

For a moment there was an awkward silence. "Would you like something to drink before we leave?" she finally offered, having no idea when she'd made the conscious decision to actually go with him. "There's some wine," she continued, resisting the urge to take a step away from his powerful frame. "Or I could make herb tea. I don't keep hard liquor on hand."

He smiled down at her, the dimple in his cheek appearing briefly. "I can live without hard liquor," he said. "But a glass of wine sounds nice."

Cassie found the rough edges to his deep voice fascinating. After a moment she realized that he'd stopped talking, and his expression was turning puzzled at her silent scrutiny.

"Please sit down," she invited hastily. "I'll put this in water and get our wine."

As she moved toward the kitchen, Crystal, the braver of her two cats, sidled past. Remembering Jack's dark slacks, Cassie turned back to warn him, then she pressed her lips together. It would be interesting to see how a man who polluted the atmosphere with poisonous chemicals would treat animals. With quick movements, she put the rose in a bud vase and reached into the fridge for the wine she'd placed there between painting her toenails and ironing her blouse.

As she was pouring two glasses, Cassie's hand shook, spilling several drops on the counter. Some form of female radar raised the hairs at the back of her neck, alerting her that Jack had walked up behind her.

"Any more where this one came from?" he asked, his voice casual. As Cassie turned she came eye to eye with Crystal, who was draped across Jack's shoulder as comfortably as if she'd been there for hours.

"She'll shed all over you," Cassie warned him, staring at the purring animal who loved heights but usually ignored strangers.

"It'll brush off," Jack answered easily as Blake, no doubt reassured by Crystal's acceptance of the tall human, rubbed against one navy blue leg.

Shrugging, Cassie finished pouring the wine as Jack stooped to pat Blake. Crystal jumped down and rubbed a cloud of light hairs against his other leg. Giving her a final pat as Cassie admired his thick hair, Jack brushed at his pants, then straightened and reached to accept the glass Cassie held out. She allowed him one grudging point for kindness to animals.

His lazy smile as his long fingers curled around the glass made Cassie wonder if making friends with the pets was part of some elaborate, time-tested seduction plan. In her book, the cats' capitulation didn't erase the fact that Jack was in a business she considered criminal. Still, he did seem to have a good side, she admitted to herself, trying to ignore the way her heartbeat faltered and then tripped along in double time whenever their gazes met.

They stood facing each other, holding their wine. Jack stared intently, and something unspoken passed between them. The walls of Cassie's composure began to melt and collapse upon themselves, and her legs turned to peanut butter.

"Here's to a very interesting relationship." His voice was a soft rasp as he touched his glass to hers.

It took total concentration to keep her hand from shaking. "I think you mean an interesting evening," she corrected in an astringent tone before sipping the rosy liquid. She was painfully aware that her gaze had shifted away from his. Coward, she accused herself silently.

"That, too," he agreed as she finally forced herself to look up at him. His smile was slightly too predatory for Cassie's peace of mind. Helplessly fascinated, she watched as he tipped his head back and the long swallow of wine rippled down his throat.

A warm feeling stole through Cassie, and she shifted nervously. Blake's strident cry of protest made her jump and almost drop her glass. She had stepped squarely on the cat's tail.

By the time they'd finished dinner at the new restaurant, she'd begun to relax, aided no doubt by the easy stream of small talk that Jack kept going with no apparent effort.

They discovered that they had both grown up in Sacramento before moving to Palmerton. Jack had worked at a series of odd jobs during high school while Cassie's spare time had been spent taking piano lessons and running around with her friends. It was later that she'd first gotten involved in several causes. After graduation, Jack had been busy starting his own business. No wonder their paths had never crossed.

Comparing notes about acquaintances and favorite haunts back in Sacramento had propelled them through dessert. Jack mentioned briefly that he'd spent one summer with an uncle in Albuquerque, describing the man and the sun-washed environment with enthusiasm. After dinner Jack and Cassie moved to the lounge where a small band was playing.

Cassie told herself she'd agreed to prolong the evening with dancing only because she hadn't had a chance to bring up the problem of Jack's spraying his parents' property. So far they had both avoided the subject of work. Now she was finding that circling the floor slowly in his embrace while the pleasantly masculine aroma of his cologne filled her senses was even less conducive to a serious conversation than sitting across the table had been.

His arms cradled her as if she were the frailest butterfly. One of her hands rested lightly on his wide shoulder and the other was tucked into his. Even so, Jack's body kept brushing against hers in repeated, teasing contact as they moved to the slow, seductive music. His body heat and the warm touch of his hand entwined with hers distracted Cassie until she began to forget the reason she was there.

When he urged her closer she didn't resist. His hard arms tightened and his breathing thinned. Her own breath rasped against lungs that almost refused to function.

After several moments he drew her hands around his neck and placed his at her waist. Cassie tipped her head back and peeped up at him through the thickness of her lashes. The movement of her head alerted him to her scrutiny, and his blue eyes blazed back at her.

She looked away in confusion, missing a step. His large hands tightened on her waist as she stumbled against his big frame, her breasts flattening onto his broad chest. The sharp intake of his breath was a gratifying sound, but then Cassie felt the silky brush of his mustache quiver against her temple in a gentle kiss. Things were rapidly getting out of hand.

As Jack's mouth touched her skin and he inhaled the delicate scent of her hair, he realized that it was time to put some distance between them. Everything about Cassie, from her appearance to the prickles in her personality to the deep softness of her voice, attracted him on a multitude of levels. Still, he hadn't forgotten their first meeting, and he meant to proceed with caution.

Jack loosened his hold and shifted slightly away from her slim body. Then, with mingled relief and disappointment, he heard the dying notes of the song and dropped his arms.

Glancing at his thin gold watch as he escorted her back to their table, he was surprised to see the time. "I suppose we'd better think about going," he said with reluctance. "Even though I hate for the evening to end."

Cassie nodded, and he wasn't sure if she was agreeing that they should leave or that she was also sorry the hours had flown. Noticing the smile on her soft mouth, he began to wonder how she would react if he tried to kiss her good-night. Somehow during the evening, kissing Cassie had moved to the top of his list of things he most wanted to accomplish in life.

They had talked during dinner, but Cassie had held a lot of herself back. That intrigued him, and he warmed to the challenge of exploring the complexities of her personality. She did seem perfectly rational, and after their bizarre first meeting he was grateful for that.

He thought again of kissing her and felt a tremor go through him. Even though Cassie seemed more reserved than many of the women he'd known, he became determined to get to know her better. Failure of any kind had no place in his vocabulary. Jack didn't think of himself as a ladies' man when he thought about it at all, but he'd never had any trouble capturing the interest of someone he wanted. And he wanted Cassie.

Sitting in the roomy cab of Jack's green truck during the drive back to her house, Cassie debated whether to ask him in. The strong attraction that had been building all evening warred with her natural reserve. She'd always been cautious in her relationships with men, perhaps because it had been so easy to keep them at arm's length—until now.

Cassie had assumed that someday a man who was perfect for her in every way would come along. It had never occurred to her that she might be fatally attracted to someone who was all wrong. Physical awareness of each other didn't cancel out the total opposition in their basic ideals, but it was more than idle curiosity that made her wonder what Jack's kiss would taste like and how his muscular arms would feel wrapped around her in a romantic embrace. That was reason enough to leave him on the other side of her front door, the sensible part of her personality whispered. Except for the fact that they hadn't yet discussed the spraying, she would be better off if she stayed away from him.

They were almost to her street. Perhaps they could discuss the subject now. Cassie glanced at Jack in the dim glow from the dash. His features were ruggedly attractive, the light illuminating his high cheekbones and strong jaw.

He glanced at her and she bit her lip, not sure how to begin.

"What's troubling you?" he asked, shattering the silence. "I can feel the tension clear over here."

When she had buckled her seat belt, she'd ignored the one in the middle of the wide bench seat, choosing instead to sit next to the passenger door. A perverse grin had tickled the corners of her mouth at his frown of annoyance.

"I'm strapped in," he continued. "I couldn't pounce on you even if I wanted to, so what's the problem?" His tone implied that he had no desire to do so.

"I wondered what you were going to do about spraying your folks' yard," she blurted, ignoring his provocative comment.

This must be what is known as a pregnant pause, Cassie thought after a long moment crawled by with no reply from Jack. She could almost feel his brain working over what she'd said.

"Is that why you went out with me tonight?" he finally asked. "To save the environment?" There was a note of hurt disbelief in his voice that Cassie assumed she must be imagining, and she could feel the force of his gaze before the road reclaimed his attention.

She wasn't sure what to say. Men who looked like Jack Hoffman didn't get their egos dented so easily, did they?

While she hesitated, he swore softly. "I'll be damned," he muttered half to himself. "That's a new one. It certainly is." Shaking his head, he pulled into her driveway and shut off the engine.

The step down from the cab was a long one. Cassie had a choice of either accepting his assistance or looking like a complete idiot. There was temper in his touch when his hands closed around her waist, and he probably wished it was her neck between his fingers, she thought as he clasped her. Her own hands gripped his shoulders as he set her down as lightly as a bit of dandelion fluff.

She stiffened, anticipating a pass. When it didn't come, the unexpected taste of disappointment pursed her mouth. As they walked past her car, he glanced at it but didn't comment. He might have decided to rush the evening to a close, but Cassie still meant to talk.

Her gaze followed his to the darkened house next door. "I almost expected Mom to be waiting up for us," he whispered, obviously trying to lighten the mood, "asking how the evening went."

Cassie chuckled softly, surprised at his change in attitude. "I know what you mean. I can't count the number of times Mother has asked me home to dinner and I've discovered someone's son seated across the table from me."

They paused at her front door, and she fished in her purse for her house key.

"You, too?" Jack took the key from her hand and unlocked the door. "Heaven help us if our mothers ever meet," he said, stepping aside and then following her in. He had shut the door behind him before Cassie had a chance to say a word.

Confused, she stooped to pet the cats, who greeted them noisily. "Feeding time," she explained over their loud cries.

"I wouldn't want to be the cause of them missing a meal," Jack replied, then glanced into the living room.

"Please sit down," Cassie said, feeling as if control of the situation had been snatched away. "I'll only be a minute."

Giving the cats food and water, she shut them in the laundry room off the kitchen. When she returned to the front of the house, Jack was sitting on the floral-printed couch, one arm flung across the back. At least he hadn't removed his jacket, but she noticed that his tie was loosened. Make yourself at home, she thought grumpily.

"Coffee?"

"Great."

"It's only instant," she cautioned, hoping to discourage him. "And decaffeinated."

"That's fine." He grinned as if he recognized her irritation and found it amusing.

Jack was watching her carefully when she returned with a wicker tray. He shifted on the couch, making room for her. If she'd only gone out with him to preach her notions of an organic world, she'd find he didn't discourage easily, he told himself grimly. Back stiff, she perched rigidly on the edge of the couch, making him smile.

"I thought you'd be a vegetarian," he said, referring to dinner as she handed him a steaming mug.

"Why?" She looked startled at his choice of topic.

"Just a guess. You surprised me when you ordered the chicken. Don't they fatten them with steroids to make them bigger?"

Her cheeks grew pink and her lashes swooped down to hide the expression in her eyes. "Actually, I did entertain the notion of being a vegetarian once," she confessed. "It was during my idealistic college days."

"Go on," he urged, thinking that she was still too idealistic in some areas for his taste.

"It was during the same period that I was picketing the slaughter of baby seals and contributing a large part of my allowance to environmental action organizations. I thought then that we could really change the world." Sighing, she seemed to shake herself before she continued.

"Actually, I'm addicted to junk food," she confessed, surprised at how much she had revealed about herself, and alert to his changing expression.

"You mean you don't eat all that healthy stuff you grow?"

"Oh, yes, I do. But I still find room for tacos, hamburgers, pizza—"

"Stop," he groaned, patting his stomach, "or we'll have to find a drive-in that hasn't closed yet."

"You, too?" she questioned. He looked so disgustingly healthy. But he was probably the type who gave no thought to salt intake or cholesterol levels. At least *she* had to wrestle pangs of guilt when she was overindulging, even if they weren't strong enough to stop her.

"Me, too," he replied. "And I don't even care what it's been sprayed with."

The smile faded from her face, and he cursed himself silently. He should have known better than to poke fun at one of her pet causes.

Cassie stood up, too annoyed at his remark to try to discuss the subject that had been at the back of her mind all evening. What was the point, anyway? He obviously thought the whole thing was a laughing matter.

Jack set down his mug and stood, too. His eyes had darkened and his mouth thinned under the bushy mustache. "I'm sorry," he said. "That was clumsy of me. I know you take your beliefs seriously."

His apology surprised Cassie, but did little to mollify her ruffled feelings. "It's late," she said. "I'm sure you have more . . . work to do tomorrow." The pause was deliberate.

Jack wondered what word she had been about to use. Poisoning? Genocide? Mass murder? He sighed and ran a hand through the layers of blond hair, disrupting its casual style. Tonight was beyond salvaging. Best to retreat and regroup.

"Good night," he said brusquely, heading for the door.

Some shadow in his blue eyes made Cassie feel mean and petty for the way she'd been acting. She put a hand on his sleeve, stopping him as surely as if she'd thrown a body block. He turned to her. For a moment he stared as if weighing an important decision. Then he muttered something under his breath and pulled her into his arms.

When he lowered his head to hers, the touch of his mouth was as gentle as his embrace was powerful. The silky caress of his mustache tickled pleasantly as his lips brushed back and forth. Then his mouth heated, sending shivers of reaction down Cassie's spine. Without conscious thought, she slid her arms around his neck and melted against him.

When Jack felt her response, his mouth hardened and he took her lips with new urgency. Flames danced behind his closed lids, and when he finally lifted his mouth, his chest rose and fell rapidly beneath the warmth of her hands.

"Good night," he repeated suddenly, his voice thick and strained.

Cassie looked into his closed expression, surprised and a little hurt that he could walk away so abruptly after the kiss they had just shared. Only a prickly sense of pride enabled her to remain silent and not call him back as he went out the door.

In moments she heard the subdued rumble of his truck engine. Dazed, she tried to make sense of the force that had just arced between them like a bolt of lightning. Kissing Jack had been a real mistake. It had satisfied her curiosity on one level but was also responsible for opening up a whole new can of worms.

The next morning, when Cassie returned from town, her mother's silver BMW was sitting in the driveway. The front door of the house was locked, and Cassie went through the house to the backyard in search of her. As soon as she opened the sliding door, the sound of voices caught her attention, and she glanced over to Mattie's. What Cassie saw made her blood run cold.

It was a nightmarish coincidence that Cassie's mother, the determined, incurable matchmaker she'd hoped would never meet Jack's equally meddlesome parent, was sitting on Mattie's deck sipping what looked like iced tea.

For a moment, Cassie contemplated closing the door very quietly and retreating to her room, preferably to hide in the closet with a favorite old teddy bear, but there was no point in postponing the inevitable. Maybe, just maybe, they had not gotten around to discussing Mattie's son and Virginia's daughter and the fact that the two of them had gone out together.

Palms damp, Cassie walked to the fence. "Hi, Mom," she called, forcing a note of welcome into her voice.

"Cassie, darling," her mother exclaimed in reply. "Mattie was just filling me in. You didn't tell me you had a new boyfriend."

Chapter Three

Cassie groaned as her mother's words made her go pink with embarrassment. As much as she wanted to disabuse her mother, Cassie swallowed her scorching reply. She couldn't say anything bad about Jack in front of Mattie, and her feelings about him were too mixed up to explain, anyway.

"He's not really a boyfriend," she said instead as her mother walked over to the fence. "We've only been out once." Her gaze shifted to her neighbor. "He's just a friend," Cassie said to his mother.

"Oh, give it time, dear," Mattie replied in a lilting voice. "I'm sure Jack will be calling you again soon."

Cassie peered at her sharply, wondering where the older woman had gotten her information. Had she already been discussing Cassie with her son, or was her confident remark just a product of wishful thinking?

I'm not so sure that he'll be calling, Cassie thought, surprised at the twinge of disappointment that closely followed her unspoken opinion.

"I see you two met," she observed lamely, her smile weak.

"I was waiting for you on the porch, and Mattie invited me over," Virginia Culpepper said. "We've had such a lovely visit."

"I'll bet," Cassie said under her breath. She eyed the two women suspiciously as a chilly feeling of uneasiness trickled down her spine.

"I'll be over in a minute," her mother said, walking along the fence with Mattie while they began to chat about a particular kind of tree rose that grew by the kitchen window.

Cassie went back through her house. She knew she hadn't heard the last about her "new boyfriend." Belatedly she wondered what new highs Mattie's blood pressure would hit when she found out the truth about the big romance. Surely Jack would waste no time in setting her straight.

Cassie's mother was long gone with a half-pint of ladybugs to control the aphids on her roses, and it was getting dark when Cassie heard a muffled thud and what sounded like a string of curses through the open window to her backyard. She pushed the chair back from her desk, where she'd been typing the next week's gardening column: questions and answers about the dangers of commercial pesticides. A thick reference book from the library was open beside her.

Before she reached the kitchen, there was a tap on the sliding door. Crystal raced past her, a low growl rolling from her throat.

Just what I need, Cassie thought as she watched Crystal skid to a stop and arch her back. An attack cat. A seven pound attack cat.

As she glanced around for a potential weapon, wondering about a burglar polite enough to knock, a familiar figure appeared at the glass door.

It was Jack Hoffman!

She unlocked the door and slid it open. "What are you—"

"Shhh!" he said in a hoarse whisper. "Let me in."

Too surprised to protest, Cassie stepped back, almost falling over the cat.

"What are you doing here?" she repeated, echoing his whisper. Then, noticing a thin scrape along his cheek, she exclaimed, "You're hurt!"

"I tore my pants, too," he said, indicating a three-cornered rip on his knee.

"How on earth did you do that, and why are you sneaking to my back door like a burglar?"

"My folks are sitting in their front yard," he said. "I almost didn't see them in the dusk, and it's a miracle they didn't notice my truck go past."

"I don't understand."

"I parked down the street and walked along the far side of your fence. It was when I was climbing over that I caught my jeans on a nail and fell."

Cassie burst out laughing. "If this is some kind of a bid for sympathy, it's not working," she finally managed between giggles. "I still don't know why you didn't just pull into the driveway."

Jack let out an exasperated sigh, touching one cautious finger to the scratch on his face. "I'm bleeding," he said, paling at the bright smear on his fingertip. Stepping around her, he sat down heavily on a kitchen chair.

"Want a bandage? I'm afraid that all I have is Pink Panther. They were on sale."

Jack shook his head, beginning to feel foolish. "I suppose you'd better put some antiseptic on it, though, if you have any." He narrowed his eyes suspiciously. "You aren't into natural healing, are you?" Lord only knew what smelly concoction she might try to put on the small wound.

The sight of blood made Jack queasy, especially when it was his own. Taking a deep breath, he checked his knee. It was unscathed beneath the rip in the denim.

Cassie shook her head, still grinning. "I have the stuff that comes in a bottle and turns orange on your skin. Good enough?" she asked.

"Does it sting?"

"Only if you've been a bad boy," she said in a teasing voice as she turned away. Her laughter drifted behind her as she went into the bathroom and opened the medicine cabinet.

Jack made a face at the cat who was staring at him, and touched the scratch again. It had become sticky.

As Cassie dabbed it with iodine, she asked again why he'd chosen such an unorthodox method of arriving at her house.

"Are you kidding?" he exclaimed, twisting one end of his mustache as he hunched his broad shoulders and glanced out the window. "Have you talked to my mother since we went out?"

"Only briefly," Cassie replied, remembering the encounter that afternoon. All her explanations about herself and Jack had fallen on deaf ears, and her own mother was dying to meet him. She'd even expressed disappointment that Jack's sister was already married, saying that from the way Mattie had described Karen she sounded perfect for Cassie's brother, Tom.

"Mom has us engaged, at the very least," Jack continued. "I had to tell her we hadn't hit it off at all, just to dissuade her from reserving the main room at their club for the party."

"That was the truth," Cassie snapped, remembering that she wasn't supposed to like this man. "We didn't hit it off."

At the disbelieving smirk on Jack's face, her gaze fell, heat filling her cheeks. Just because she'd responded to his kiss didn't mean she had to like him, she argued silently with herself.

"What party?" she asked suddenly, remembering the rest of what he'd said.

"Our engagement party," he answered dryly.

"Oh, Lord."

"That's something like what I said," he drawled, remembering that his mother had admonished him for his language when he'd commented rather heatedly on her suggestion. The last thing he was looking for was a fiancée. No, the last thing was a wife, handpicked by his mother. The next to last was a fiancée. When he'd said that, Mattie had laughed and told him not to fight it. Even now, he could still feel the rope burn from an imaginary noose.

"Did you hurt your neck when you fell?" Cassie asked anxiously when she saw him rubbing it.

"What? Er, no, it's fine." Jack's hand dropped. "Couldn't you close the curtains?" he requested after another nervous glance at the window. "And now do you understand why I climbed your fence?"

"I'm beginning to," Cassie replied, pulling down the shade on the Hoffman side of the kitchen. "What I don't understand is why you came by at all."

For a moment Jack just looked at her, expression unreadable. Then he pulled her across his thighs and muttered, "For this," before his mouth covered hers.

Any protest she might have uttered died a quick death under the demands he made. Her hands fluttered briefly before circling his neck, and her lips parted at his gentle urgency. A hard shudder went through his big body as she wiggled on his lap trying to get closer, and the spark between them flared as quickly as it had the first time.

Jack's tongue touched hers, stroking, then he retreated and nibbled at her lips. When he pulled away, his cheeks were flushed and his eyes had darkened to the color of a night sky.

"You're really very special," he said, voice thickened.

Cassie pulled out of his embrace, shaking her head in denial of his words. "This is all wrong," she exclaimed as she stood up and turned away, trembling. Confusion boiled within her. How could she be so totally drawn to someone whose basic beliefs were so vastly different from her own?

The chair scraped back as Jack straightened to his full, imposing height. His hands on her shoulders turned her gently back to face him, then he ran a finger along the line of her jaw and tucked it under her chin, tipping her head back.

"Why?" he questioned harshly. "Why is it wrong?"

Jack felt a nameless hunger as he stared down at her, trying to read the thoughts concealed behind her brown eyes.

"Because," she said, pulling away, "I'm 'Save the Seals' and you're 'Rape the Earth.'"

"That's a little strong," he muttered, jamming his hands into his pockets to keep from reaching out and shaking her. It took iron control to subdue the strong emotions that flowed through him as they faced each other. He wouldn't have guessed in a hundred years what filling in for one of his drivers would lead to, and he wished passionately that he and Cassie had met under different circumstances. Knowing that anger would only make things worse between them, he groped for the right words to explain his position, a position he'd given no thought to until a few days before.

"I'm convinced that the chemicals I use are safe," he finally said, recalling the former owner's assurances and the confident words of the instructional booklet he'd read. "If I didn't believe that, I'd close down the business tomorrow."

"That's a thought."

He frowned but his words had given Cassie a thread of hope. Perhaps she could prove to him somehow that he was wrong. Determined, she placed a hand on his bare arm.

She felt little bumps under her fingers. Glancing down, she noticed the faint, pink rash that covered his forearms. "What's that?" She rubbed his arm lightly.

Scratching at the reddened skin, he said, "I don't know. I think I'm allergic to your cats."

"How long have you had the rash?"

"Since I came over here last time. Perhaps you'll have to start visiting my apartment, instead," he suggested, a wicked light in his eyes as he made a grab for her.

Cassie avoided his hand, stifling reluctant laughter. "Nice try, Hoffman," she said. "You probably put something on your arms deliberately, but you're to be congratulated for an approach I haven't heard before."

Jack just shrugged and smiled before sliding his hands around her waist. This time Cassie didn't pull away. "We have to work out our differences," he said softly, urging her close. "I refuse to give up."

His possessive words and the warmth of him pressed against her made Cassie's objections scatter like dry leaves before a hot wind. She didn't concur, but she didn't argue with him as they stood together in a loose embrace.

"And," Jack added, humor coloring his deep voice, "we have to do it all while avoiding our mothers."

Cassie agreed emphatically right before his mouth covered hers in a sensuous assault that left her heart pounding and her senses clamoring for more. Blake meowed several times, then as they continued to ignore him he made an almost human sound of disgust and padded silently away.

Jack left a few moments later, after promising to call Cassie during the week. Too befuddled by his last kiss to attempt to dissuade him, she promised herself that she would set him straight the very next chance she had.

It was dark and the front yard next door was empty as he walked boldly down the driveway, after muttering that he felt like a criminal or a cheating husband. Cassie didn't like sneaking around, either, but it was easier than dealing with their mothers.

She watched his tall frame disappear into the night. If they were to continue seeing each other, which of course was impossible, there would be no way they'd be able to keep it a secret.

Remembering how persistent her mother could be, Cassie vowed to keep Jack Hoffman from coming anywhere near her house, for any reason. If they did continue to meet, it would have to be across the state line, just in case.

Glad she wouldn't have to go to such elaborate lengths for a man she didn't even like, Cassie locked the front door and prepared for bed. The pickers were bringing in more ladybugs the next day, and she would have to get everything set up early for the sorting and washing.

Not that she actually washed the little red beetles, but they were sprayed with water when she packed them into cold storage. It gave the ladybugs a drink before the early, artificial hibernation that would hold them for shipping.

At some moment before sleep claimed her, Cassie's thoughts wandered from the next day's duties to the way Jack had kissed her that evening. Her dreams were of a very male, very sexy human, and the cute little bugs who were supposed to bring good luck were temporarily forgotten.

Early the next morning, while Cassie was busy in her converted garage, Jack was giving last-minute instructions to his extremely pregnant secretary.

"I don't know why it's so difficult to find an experienced replacement for Ralph," he grumbled, flipping quickly through the mail. "And pretty soon you'll be gone, too."

"I'll be back when Junior here is a little bigger, if the new owner will have me," Donna answered, pausing to give her stomach an affectionate pat before slitting another envelope. "You're a good boss to work for, and I'm sorry you're selling the business again so quickly." She sighed before picking up another envelope. "Actually, I'd love to stay home with my baby, but we'll never be able to buy a house if I don't work awhile longer."

Jack nodded, understanding her reasoning. "I'll make your job a condition of the sale," he said. "Don't worry about it, but I do have to find a temporary replacement for you."

"Shall I call one of the agencies?"

He thought a minute, then agreed. "Yeah, that's a good idea. Find someone who can type with more than two fingers and count to ten, okay? I have some calls to make, and then I'll take care of these jobs that Juan won't have time for." He picked up a clipboard, closing his office door behind him.

After Jack had settled himself behind the scarred wooden desk and looked at the list of calls, several minutes passed before he reached for the phone. By the time he did, it was difficult to banish the daydream of kissing Cassie that made him shift uncomfortably in the worn chair.

It was five hours later that the ringing of her telephone interrupted Cassie's concentration and made her glance at her watch. No wonder she was starved!

"How about meeting me for a late lunch?" asked a husky male voice when she answered. Totally unprepared for the call from Jack, she took a moment to compose herself before answering. As she was about to refuse, her stomach rumbled beseechingly.

"Sure," she said instead, ignoring the inner voice that told her she was nuts. "But only if it's come as you are." She was too hungry to take the time for major repairs. If Jack couldn't take her at her worst, perhaps he'd lose interest.

"Great," he replied. "I don't have much time, but I wanted to see you."

He named a taco stand close to Cassie's, and she promised to be there in twenty minutes. That would give her time for a quick wash and a moment to comb her hair. She even managed to block out any second thoughts until she'd pulled up in front of Chico's Tacos.

Jack's green pickup was already there, and he was waiting at an outdoor table in the shade. Cassie wondered what he'd done with the white tank truck.

Pride and some deeper emotion made Cassie's cheeks flush when Jack stood and walked toward her. Even in low riding jeans and a casual shirt, almost completely unbuttoned against the heat, he looked better than any other man there. Cassie noticed the admiring glances that followed him as he walked past a group of women in office clothes, but Jack seemed oblivious to their interest. His gaze remained firmly fixed on Cassie.

When they were face-to-face, he smiled and greeted her in a husky voice. "I'm glad you could come," he said, running one knuckle down her cheek and crooking it under her chin.

"Me, too," she admitted, voice faint. Awareness made her throat close up and her skin tingle in response to his casual caress.

Breaking the sizzling contact of their gazes, she glanced up at his baseball cap. It bore the name of a popular brand of fertilizer that had been linked with cancer in laboratory animals. She frowned, the tentative contact between them dissolving.

Seeing her stiffen, Jack was at first puzzled. Then, following the direction of her gaze, he yanked off the offending cap and studied it briefly. Muttering a short, succinct curse, he stuffed the hat into a back pocket and ran a hand through his straight hair. After his attempt to smooth it, he glared down at Cassie impatiently. She looked ready to bolt at the slightest excuse.

"Let's order some of that junk food we both love," he said tightly, "then we'll have a nice conversation about the weather or our favorite TV programs."

"Read any good books lately?" Cassie inquired in response to his grim attempt at humor as he grabbed her elbow and pulled her toward the line at the window of the taco stand.

Grinning, Jack bent toward her and spoke softly into her ear. "Come over to my place," he drawled as he draped a muscular arm across her shoulders, "and I'll show you my bookshelves."

Cassie's toes curled in the confines of her leather sandals, and goose bumps popped up along her arms despite the heat. Her whole body came to attention as his breath tickled the sensitive skin of her neck. Taking a deep gulp of air that riveted his interested gaze on the thrust of her breasts against the thin fabric of her plaid shirt, she attempted a cool smile. If it was a little ragged around the edges, he seemed not to notice.

The atmosphere between them was light and teasing through lunch. By silent agreement they avoided any topic that would have the slightest chance of being controversial. Cassie was glad to see that the scrape on his face had scabbed over and showed no sign of infection. When she asked about his knee, he insisted on rolling up his pant leg to show her the bruise.

Cassie was used to the sight of men's legs in all manner of shorts and cutoffs, but the casual way Jack exposed his powerful limb, deeply tanned and dusted with golden hair, made her mouth go dry. She barely glanced at the faint, blue mark he indicated before looking away in confusion.

Cassie was beginning to feel like one of her own lady-bugs, tumbled end over end as she was sucked deeper into the harvester's bag.

"You ready?"

Cassie blinked in confusion, then looked down at the empty wrappings. "Yes!"

As Jack walked her to the red Volkswagen, he dropped their garbage into the trash barrel.

Gripping the car door handle, he paused.

"How about spending the day with me tomorrow? I've got something special in mind, and I'd like to share it with you."

Despite Cassie's questions, he refused to elaborate, only asking that she trust him. As she gazed up into his eyes, narrowed against the bright sunlight and screened by thick lashes, trusting him was absurdly easy. Before she realized what she was doing, she'd agreed. His only comment was to suggest that she dress casually.

Then he opened her door, bending to cover her lips with a quick kiss that left Cassie hungry for more.

"Until tomorrow," he said. "I'll pick you up at ten."

"What about your parents?" Cassie asked, remembering his near disastrous efforts to avoid them the night before.

A wicked light filled his eyes. "I didn't invite them," he said.

Cassie pushed at him with the flat of her hand. "You know what I meant."

"I already checked," he replied as he lifted her hand and dusted the knuckles with his mustache. "They're leaving early for Tahoe, and they're staying overnight with friends."

A small "oh" of reply pushed past the lump that had suddenly found a home in Cassie's throat. Not knowing what else to say, she mumbled her thanks for lunch and slid behind the wheel of her bizarrely painted car. With a final wave, she started the engine and shifted into gear. It took a lot of willpower to resist the urge to sit and watch Jack stride over to his truck. She found the graceful way his big body moved infinitely fascinating. Some deeply rooted feminine instinct told Cassie that ten o'clock the next morning would take forever to arrive.

When the appointed time finally did crawl around, she was still slightly groggy from a night of tossing and turning. She'd given up trying to sleep shortly after dawn, and had managed to finish writing next week's gardening column while drinking three cups of coffee. She almost wished it wasn't decaffeinated.

The cats' running conversation irritated her, and she stuffed them outside before exchanging her pink gingham duster for jeans and a striped polo shirt. She placed a light windbreaker and a straw hat to shield her from the sun next to her canvas purse, and when the doorbell rang she was nibbling a slice of dry toast made from whole grain bread she'd baked herself. Dumping the toast in the trash, she flew to the front door, then took a deep, steadying breath and opened it slowly.

Jack, clad in faded jeans and a striped shirt with the sleeves rolled up, was holding a cat under each arm. "My welcoming committee," he said, setting Blake and Crystal down on the porch.

They both slithered past Cassie into the relative coolness of the house. On his way past her, Blake mouthed what was probably a Siamese swearword. When Jack rested his hands lightly on her shoulders, Cassie noticed that the rash on his forearms was redder than it had been, but the scrape on his face had almost healed.

He pushed her gently back into the house, his blue eyes dark with the first stirrings of interest. Smiling, Cassie glanced past him to see if any neighbors were about to witness their kiss of welcome, when her attention was caught and held by the apparition parked there. Her feet stopped moving and her mouth dropped open.

"There's a burgundy limousine in the driveway," she stammered, ducking out of Jack's embrace.

"I know," he said as he recaptured her and his head lowered.

"Wait!" Cassie commanded, turning her face so that his kiss landed harmlessly on her cheek. "There's a man in a chauffeur's uniform standing next to the limo."

"I know," Jack repeated, one hand cupping her chin as he again attempted to kiss her.

"But, but . . ." Cassie sputtered.

Jack's arms fell away from her and he sighed. "Okay," he finally said, stepping back. "I rented the limo and I rented the chauffeur. *Now* can I have a kiss, or do you have some questions about the picnic basket in the back seat?"

"I didn't know there was a picnic basket in the back seat," Cassie said.

"Good." Jack's mouth settled on hers and he kissed her very thoroughly, driving Cassie's questions right out of her head. When he finally released her from the branding possession of his lips, she clung to him weakly, silently commanding her rubbery legs to support her. They finally cooperated and she released the handfuls of his shirtfront she hadn't even realized she'd been gripping.

Peering down into her slightly glazed brown eyes, Jack allowed himself a smile of pleasure before scooping up her purse, jacket and hat. "This all?" he asked, brimming with male satisfaction at Cassie's obvious difficulty in forming even a simple answer to his question.

"Mmm," she finally managed, blinking several times.

"Lock your door," he instructed patiently, willing his own response to the feel of her delightfully soft body back to manageable levels.

Cassie's gaze cleared and she gave her head a tiny shake. After instructing the cats to behave, she followed Jack to the waiting limo. The chauffeur opened the back door, and Jack handed her into its luxurious interior.

As Cassie slid over, waiting for Jack to join her on the maroon leather seat, she looked around curiously. Questions filled her mind and threatened to spill from her lips, but she sensed that asking would be futile. Jack would clue her in when he was good and ready. In the meantime, she meant to enjoy every minute of the unexpected outing. The desire to know their destination was pushed aside as Jack settled in beside her and pushed a button. A burgundy satin curtain slid soundlessly across the glass partition that separated them from the driver's compartment. That, along with the tinted windows, surrounded them in a cocoon of privacy.

Cassie barely had time to notice the wicker picnic basket that rested on the jump seat across from them before Jack slid an arm behind her.

"Our adventure begins," he murmured as his fingers toyed with a strand of her dark hair.

Cassie's pulses began to tap-dance as she absorbed the aroma of the leather interior mixed with Jack's own enticing male scent. The car was moving, but she had lost interest in which way they were headed. Her senses were filled by Jack's presence, the feel of his fingers tugging gently on her hair and the sight of his blue eyes staring into hers. A tiny sigh left her parted lips as her hand stole around his neck.

Urging his head down, she touched her mouth to his, delighting in his response. A heady feeling of power made her bold. There was something about the car and the sense of unreal isolation that fueled a reckless feeling of aggressiveness. The neatly trimmed edge of his golden mustache tickled her lips, and she could feel the muscles of his arm tensing beneath her hand. She allowed the very tip of her tongue to touch his lightly as she teased him further.

For endless moments, Jack seemed not even to breathe as he held himself rigidly still beneath her caresses. Cassie's exploring fingers traced along the edge of his collar, lightly scoring his hot, damp skin with her nails.

Suddenly Jack's control snapped like the steel bands surrounding a packing crate, and he crushed her to his wide chest. "Little minx," he rasped, right before he kissed her with burning male authority. When his lips worked their magic, Cassie began to melt like hot candle wax and her fingers buried themselves in his hair.

Jack began suddenly to pull away, and Cassie tightened her arms around his neck. She moaned and buried her hot face into his shoulder.

"We're here, honey," he said, the thickness of his voice betraying his own desire. His hands became soothing as he stroked her arms. When the door was opened from the outside, Cassie's breathing had almost returned to normal, but she was still stunned by the powerful emotions Jack made her feel.

She blinked owlishly into the sun's brightness. Jack got out and helped her from the car before ducking back in to grab the picnic basket. Absently, Cassie clutched her purse and hat while her brain boggled at the sight looming before her wide eyes.

Like a wild stallion eager to be free, a huge hot-air balloon banded in purple-and-yellow stripes strained at the ropes that tethered it, while towering over the wicker gondola festooned with ballast. An attendant was in the basket, doing something to the flames that were shooting up into the mouth of the huge balloon.

Cassie stared, speechless. As Jack gazed at her, she clapped her hands together in unfeigned excitement. Riding in a hot-air balloon had been a favorite fantasy of Cassie's for years. As she turned to ask him how he had guessed, he moved her gently forward.

"This is a friend of mine, Gary Hottell," he shouted over the roar of the burner. The other man nodded to Cassie, and she flashed him a rather dazed smile.

To her surprise, Gary jumped out of the gondola and slapped Jack on the back. "Have a good time," he said.

Jack said something that Cassie didn't hear, then thanked Gary and shook his hand. After putting the picnic hamper on board, Jack turned to Cassie.

"This okay with you?" he asked. "If you'd rather not, we don't have to go up."

Cassie bobbed her head. "Yes," she said, excited. "I want to go."

Jack climbed into the waist-high basket, then assisted her.

"Isn't Gary going to pilot us?" she asked Jack nervously as the other man began untying the tethers.

Jack shook his head. "No, I am," he said. "Relax, I'm qualified, and you'll be perfectly safe with me. I learned from my uncle down in Albuquerque."

As the flames roared and the balloon began a graceful ascent, Cassie thought fleetingly that she was anything but safe with Jack Hoffman.

They soared above the trees, and Jack slipped an arm around her shoulders, pulling her close. Cassie leaned back and laughed. She watched his eyes darken in response. Even though there could never be anything serious between them, she decided right then to savor the day. The wind was ruffling her hair, and Jack's solid bulk warmed her at every point their bodies touched. Sometimes there were far better things to be than safe, she thought with a tiny smile.

Chapter Four

Cassie was enjoying their ride. The fear she had always thought she'd experience so high from the ground was absent; instead breathless wonder filled her, mixed with pleasure at being with Jack.

The only sound was the occasional blast from the pressurized propane burner as Cassie looked out over the edge of the wicker basket to the rolling hills beneath them. Jack curled an arm around her waist and dropped a kiss on her temple.

"What do you think?" he asked, ignoring the way her body stiffened. "Do you like ballooning?"

She turned to look directly into his eyes, then shifted her gaze away hastily. His nearness brought the butterflies to her middle that the flight hadn't.

"I love it," she said. "I've always wanted to do this."

Beside her, Jack smiled. His fears that the ride was a crazy idea she would hate receded, and he shifted his arm to drape it across her shoulders. "I'm glad," he murmured into her ear as his fingers lightly stroked her neck. She shivered beneath his hands.

Trying to ignore his own response to her nearness, Jack tore his gaze away from her delicate profile and checked the gauges that indicated altitude, rate of ascent and the temperature inside the balloon. Despite the cooling breezes whipping at them he felt warm, and wondered what his own temperature would measure at that moment.

His free hand rested on the Up button that controlled the propane burner. A rope—the Down button that could open a side slit near the balloon's top—was close by. He watched carefully to see where they were going; it wouldn't do to land in a tree while he was distracted by his pretty passenger.

"Is this your balloon?" Cassie asked, remembering the way his friend had turned it over to him.

"Partially. Gary and I own it together. That way one of us can spot for the other. I first got interested in ballooning when I spent the summer with my uncle, but it took a while before I became licensed and could buy into a balloon of my own."

"This is wonderful," Cassie shouted, thrusting out her chin so the wind ruffled her hair with inquisitive fingers. She was supremely conscious of Jack's muscular body next to her, its affect more dizzying than the ground rushing beneath them.

As near as Cassie could tell, their landing an hour later was almost perfect. Jack set the giant balloon down with only a few bumps in a field of tall grasses by a shallow stream. After helping Cassie from the gondola, he handed over the picnic basket.

"It's heavy," he cautioned. "Let me carry it toward the water. Then if you'd help me..." He gestured upward with a tilt of his head. Sunlight gleamed on the golden strands of his hair.

"Sure." Cassie took the plaid blanket from the basket and preceded him to the stream bank, stopping at a grassy spot in the shade of a gigantic tree.

"This okay?" she asked, spreading out the blanket when he nodded.

"Perfect." The hamper dropped with a muffled thud onto the grass. When Cassie straightened he curled his fingers around her wrist, examining the fragile-looking joint with apparent interest. "Are you enjoying yourself?" There was an earnest note in his voice that surprised her.

Cassie met his inquiring gaze squarely. "Very much," she murmured. Her lack of hesitation was another surprise; she hadn't expected to enjoy herself quite so much . . . or perhaps she hadn't wanted to.

Jack was staring at her mouth intently, his thick lashes screening the intense blue of his eyes. When his gaze returned to lock with hers, its brilliance made her swallow thickly. She took a step backward.

Jack's hand dropped away and he grinned, his teeth a slash of white against his dark skin. He was really almost too good to be true, she thought distractedly. Physically he could be the star in any woman's dream, with his big, muscular body and blond hair, his pirate's mustache.

She cast about for something to say, anything to break the silence that was beginning to hum between them like the buzz from a neon sign.

Jack turned toward the balloon, oblivious to the tension holding Cassie a silent prisoner. "Come on," he said over his shoulder. "The sooner the work's done, the sooner we eat."

He showed her what he wanted her to do, and Cassie followed his instructions easily. Beneath her lashes she watched dry mouthed the way his muscles bunched while he stretched and bent, his movements as graceful as they were efficient. Unbidden, unwelcome thoughts flitted into her head like the shiny flying insect that hovered in front of her face until she brushed it away. If only her attraction to the man with her was as easy to dispose of.

They made a good team, and before long the work was done. Side by side, they walked toward the blanket in easy companionship.

"I'm starved," Jack exclaimed. "How about you?"

"Famished."

He held her hand lightly as she knelt on the blanket, then sprawled beside her.

"What's in the basket?" Cassie asked as he opened the top.

"A feast, I hope," Jack said, digging around inside. "Be a good girl and set the table." He handed her plastic plates and silverware with wooden handles.

Cassie's head jerked at his tone, and she almost said something rash. Then she eyed him closely, seeing the telltale twitch of his thick mustache.

"That's the least I can do after you provided the food," she said sweetly.

Jack glanced up and she smiled blandly. He handed her the plastic cups he'd been holding, an expression of disappointment crossing his face.

"Shouldn't you be out hunting a bear to barbecue or something?" Cassie quizzed him.

He chuckled wryly. "I forgot my bow and arrows. Guess we'll have to settle for cold chicken." He opened a container of crispy, golden pieces.

Cassie set a paper napkin by his plate as Jack busied himself taking dishes of pasta salad and marinated vegetables from the basket and opening them.

"Did you fix all this?" she asked.

"Mom did the chicken, but I got the rest at this terrific deli by my apartment."

"Do you cook?" she asked, sampling the pasta salad while Jack poured them each a glass of wine.

"When I have to. Mostly barbecue, but I haven't done any bear lately."

She returned his smile as they clinked their plastic cups together. For a few moments they ate in silence.

"How did you get into the bug business?" Jack asked, picking up a drumstick. There was a genuinely curious expression on his face as he scratched absently at the rash on his arm.

Briefly, Cassie told him about her checkered job history and the long-standing desire to make a living doing something with gardening. "The ladybugs started out as a sideline," she concluded, "but the business is getting bigger and bigger. I ship them all over the country now."

"You really shocked me when you first said you sold ladybugs. I didn't know people did that."

"Tell me more about your business," she countered, remembering with embarrassment their first meeting when she'd tried to drown him.

Jack took a sip of the dry white wine. "Nothing much to tell. After college I worked for a while, then bought a small construction company. Four years ago I got my first really big job, and we've been lucky since then."

He shifted positions, and Cassie had the impression he was uncomfortable talking about himself. "I needed to expand the yard, so I started negotiating on the vacant lot next door, but the owner wouldn't sell unless I also bought Sierra Pest Control from him. He knew he had me—I'm boxed in on three sides." He gestured with the celery stick in his hand. "The rest is history, and here we are."

Cassie made a face at his sharply edited story. "You make it sound so simple," she said. "But I bet it wasn't. You've worked hard," she guessed.

"I suppose I've put in a few long days," he agreed modestly. "This area's starting to open up, and I've helped build some new businesses that have brought jobs here."

"Development has its drawbacks, too," Cassie felt compelled to add. "The area between here and Sacramento is growing so fast. Pretty soon it will all be paved over."

"I doubt that. But the growth is important. Look at the revenue that new shopping mall has brought with it. And I'll bet you like to shop there."

Cassie was beginning to get irritated with his one-way attitude. "That shopping mall covered a field of wildflowers," she snapped. "You may not think they were important to the economy, but a lot of people liked to look at them, and kids flew kites there."

Jack found himself staring in disbelief. Wildflowers? Kites? There were more than fifty stores in that mall, all generating taxes and jobs. Who was she trying to kid with her Mary Poppins attitude that flowers were more important?

"Would you rather we all lived in mud huts so we didn't have to cut down any trees?" he asked. "Might as well go all the way."

Her mouth got a tight look about it, and her dark eyes flashed. "Don't be ridiculous. But if we keep developing every bit of empty land, future generations will have to look at books if they want to see wildflowers.''

Jack wondered if that would be so bad as long as unemployment went down. Men came by his office every day looking for work, and they weren't choosy, either. ''There will always be flowers somewhere,'' he said, growing tired of the argument.

''Just like there will always be California condors and whooping cranes?'' Her cheeks were flushed attractively.

Jack didn't want to argue with her. ''You may have a point,'' he said. ''But there are laws to regulate all that, anyway.''

Cassie stared hard, wanting to comment further. Then, after a long pause, she took a deep breath and let it out slowly. It was too nice a day to argue. Glancing down, she was surprised to see that her plate was empty. When Jack lifted two slices of cheesecake from the depths of the hamper, she shook her head and patted her stomach.

''Not for me,'' she said. ''You go ahead.''

Instead of doing that, he repacked them. ''I've had enough, too,'' he said.

''It was a lovely picnic,'' Cassie commented, helping with the mess. ''And a lovely ride.''

Closing the hamper, he leaned toward her. ''I'm glad you liked it.'' His voice was deeper, his face serious. He rose smoothly to a kneeling position and pulled Cassie up with him. His hands on her bare upper arms were warm and firm, his eyes were glowing with an inner fire, and his mouth below the thick mustache was curved into a smile. One hand came up, and his fingers traced a line along her jaw. Cassie swallowed nervously and fought the urge to moisten her suddenly dry lips as she stared up at him.

"I can't figure you out," Jack said softly. "We're like oil and water sometimes, but when we're close like this..." He paused and sighed. He was so near that his breath was like a caress in the stillness of the warm afternoon. As he leaned even closer, Cassie's eyelids fluttered helplessly downward, and she tilted her chin just enough to meet his descending mouth.

The first kiss was a gentle joining, a sweet melding. After the scantest hesitation, Cassie's hands slipped around Jack's neck, touching his sun-warmed hair. It felt like heavy silk. His mustache caressed her skin as gently as a sable brush.

His head lifted and he took a shallow breath as Cassie's eyelids fluttered open. "Your mouth is so soft," he whispered, his thick lashes filtering the light in his eyes.

As he watched her, mesmerized, Cassie's lips parted as if she, too, had felt the utter rightness of the kiss. Groaning, Jack swooped again.

The sound of an approaching car thrust its way into his consciousness, and beneath his hands Cassie's body tensed as if she also heard it.

Jack looked up, relief and irritation warring within him. Where was his usually reliable control around this complex and compelling minx? For a timeless moment he'd forgotten everything but how good she felt in his arms.

"It's the limo," he said, straightening and dropping his hands. When he glanced at the slim gold watch on his arm he could hardly believe the time. The afternoon had flown. Reluctantly he stood, offering Cassie a hand up. She scrambled to her feet, a telltale color flaming her cheeks, but she didn't meet his gaze as she quickly pulled her fingers away.

Good, he thought, at least she wasn't indifferent. Then he caught himself. Did he want her to be responsive? Did he want the attraction he felt deep within himself when he looked at her? His feelings about Cassie Culpepper were definitely confused as he turned with a frown to greet the chauffeur he'd hired.

A few moments later as Cassie sat beside him in the spacious back seat of their steel chariot, the balloon safely packed away in its own container and riding in the limo's trunk, Cassie was dealing with second thoughts of her own. How much simpler it would be if Jack's touch left her cold. Instead, one glance melted her insides and a caress turned her resolutions to mush. She didn't even want to think about what his kisses did, not with him sitting next to her.

"Why aren't you running your spraying truck today?" she asked in a quarrelsome tone, wanting to puncture the silence between them. "Surely there are more dragons left in Palmerton to slay?"

Jack's jaw tightened in reaction to her gibe, and he turned to stare down at her, his eyes frosting over. "That's the advantage of being the boss," he said. "I can take time off."

Cassie's mind whirled with questions, and she spoke without thinking. "With your construction company, you don't really need Sierra Pest Control, do you?"

Jack shifted on the soft, leather seat. "Well, I—"

"You could shut it down," Cassie continued, caught up in her idea. Her voice became edged with the excitement she was feeling. "Think of the good you'd be doing!"

All Jack's business instincts burst forth in a rush of indignation. "Shut it down? You mean just close the doors and quietly go out of business?" He couldn't believe she'd suggest such a thing. She didn't know how he'd struggled during the first years, trying to keep his fledgling company going in the face of skyrocketing interest rates, canceled contracts, strikes and other calamities. The idea of voluntarily quitting went against his basic sense of survival.

"Would you cut down a living tree?" he asked. "Pull out a healthy plant by the roots? How can you suggest such a thing?" His voice had risen, and he tried to lower it. "You don't buy a healthy business to shut it down."

Beside him, Cassie inched away, leaving a wider space between them on the leather seat. She couldn't believe she'd been rash enough to poke into his business affairs and make the suggestion she had. Jack had every right to be upset. He was obviously a proud and a hardworking man, and she had insulted his accomplishments.

Cassie hung her head, knowing how she would feel if someone suggested she terminate her mail order business and take up another line of work. Not for the first time she silently cursed her runaway tongue as she tried to think of the words to make amends.

Beside her, Jack ran agitated fingers through his hair, muttering that his accountant would have a stroke and that he had two employees to think of. Cassie felt even worse, realizing that she had totally disregarded the other people involved. She silently nibbled on her knuckle as Jack fumed.

"The business is for sale," he finally blurted just as she was about to apologize. "I never had any intentions of keeping it." His expression made it plain that he thought that solved everything.

"*Someone* will still be spreading poison," Cassie couldn't help but comment. "Even if it isn't you."

Jack muttered something unprintable before lapsing back into silence. Cassie toyed with her pierced earring, turning it around and around while she thought about what had been said. They seemed to be at an impasse. She knew she couldn't do anything about all the spraying businesses around, but it was still frustrating that, thanks to Jack Hoffman, one more would keep spreading its deadly product.

When they pulled into Cassie's driveway, she caught Jack glancing surreptitiously at the house next door, obviously relieved that his parents' car was still gone from their driveway.

"I had a very nice time," Cassie said stiffly as the chauffeur held the back door open and Jack helped her out. The presence of the uniformed attendant made her feel awkward as Jack accompanied her up the sidewalk.

"Ask me inside," he said when they stopped on the porch.

Cassie glanced at the long car, then back at his big, handsome face. It was obvious from the glittering light in his eyes that their argument hadn't deterred him totally. Cassie's cheeks grew hot; the attraction she felt toward him was far from snuffed out. Still, she was determined to fight her interest in this totally unsuitable man.

"I have a lot to do," she hedged. "Perhaps we'd better say goodbye right here."

Jack's mouth thinned in annoyance. He was tempted to push open the door she'd just unlocked and hustle her inside where he could take her in his arms and block out the angry words they'd exchanged. Such tactics weren't part of his nature. Instead, he summoned a casual smile, saying, "I have a meeting later, so I'd better go change."

Without allowing himself time to even think about touching her, he turned away and stepped off the porch.

Jack had been too busy with the construction business to bother with much of a social life, and it had been just recently that he sometimes found himself lonely in a way that stopping for a beer with the crew or a brief relationship centered on mutual physical attraction didn't appease. He might find Cassie interesting, but her cockeyed ideas would just keep getting in the way. A long, cold shower would be just as effective and a whole lot simpler.

"Uh, thanks again," she called after him, her voice hesitant. "I had a nice time."

Her expression when Jack gave a backward glance was totally gratifying, wiping out any thoughts of a cold shower. She clearly hovered between confusion and disappointment. Whistling tunelessly, he settled himself into the back seat of the rented limo. "Home, James," he said in a cheerful voice, sinking comfortably into the soft, leather seat.

As the limo backed down her driveway, Cassie allowed herself the indulgence of slamming her front door. He didn't need to give up so easily, she thought as her two cats ran out to greet her. They'd probably been sleeping the day away on the foot of her bed.

Taking a minute to give each animal a pat and a scratch around the ears, she told them, "Be glad you're both fixed. At least you don't have to deal with the opposite sex, unpredictable and unreliable bunch that they are."

Crystal began to purr and Blake flattened his ears as if he knew she'd been casting aspersions on his former gender. With a last, muttered grumble, Cassie went into the bedroom to change her clothes. The three rows of lettuce that needed weeding wouldn't wait. Well, she could always pretend the weeds she uprooted were a certain muscular hunk with laughing eyes and a thick mustache. The most irritating thing about her annoyance was not being able to analyze its cause. Why was she so upset with Jack when he'd only gone along with what she wanted?

It was several days later that Cassie told herself not for the first time how glad she was that Jack hadn't contacted her. It couldn't be his lack of attention that made her irritable, she thought, banging away at the keyboard of her computer. It must be something else: the tomato blight she was trying to control with copper dust, the houseplant Blake had knocked over, the trouble she was having writing her weekly gardening column.

She'd finally settled on a sizzling denunciation of chemical pest control, ignoring the twinges of conscience that kept plaguing her. Was Jack threatening her objectivity? She couldn't believe that she'd use her column to advance a vendetta, even subconsciously. So what if he hadn't called? She didn't want to see him again anyway.

As if in protest of the blatant untruth, the computer beeped as she held a key down too long. She'd better concentrate on what she was doing or she'd delete the whole column and have to start over. Rereading the copy, she activated the printer and got up to make lunch, glaring at the silent phone as she walked past.

Her pickers would be coming by late that afternoon with more cloth bags of ladybugs to be processed. The next few days would be busy, even though she'd already printed out mailing labels and invoices on the computer. Perhaps being busy was just what she needed to get her mind off Jack Hoffman and her silent telephone.

Both cats followed her into the kitchen, meowing hopefully. Cassie was tempted to give them a little of the cold turkey she took out to add to the salad greens but knew if she did they'd never leave her alone when she was preparing food.

"Be patient," she said. "Dinner is only a few hours away." To listen to their mournful cries one would think it had been days since they'd eaten.

She pushed Crystal out of the way with her foot. "Scoot," she said, growing irritated. "Go outside and play." Then Cassie couldn't help but grin at herself; she sounded as if she was talking to her children. For a long moment she stood at the sink, staring sightlessly out the window.

Children. Chubby little boys and girls with golden hair and bright blue eyes. When she realized where her thoughts were leading, she stomped over to the back door and let the cats out. Then she attacked a raw zucchini with her cleaver. When she did have children, they most certainly would not be little copies of the man who spent his time polluting her air! What on earth had she been thinking?

While Cassie was putting together her lunch salad, Jack was conferring with one of his foremen over thick ham sandwiches and a thermos of coffee. The strip mall they were finishing was a small job, but he liked to check on its progress from time to time. Between that and helping Juan with the orders at Sierra Pest Control, it had been a hectic week.

He'd gone to his sister's house to celebrate his brother-in-law's birthday one evening, squashing the urge to invite Cassie along. He'd known that his parents would be there, and he'd told himself it wasn't worth engaging his mother's curiosity. Maybe someday she'd lose interest in her active campaign to get him married off and breeding more grandchildren for her to spoil, but he doubted it.

The thought of kids of his own, little girls with Cassie's dark hair and sparkling eyes, made him almost spill the coffee he'd just poured into the plastic cup. Rattled, he turned his attention to John Clearwater, the job foreman, as the other man began to explain why they'd have to add more gravel trucks to the job to stay on schedule.

A half hour later, Jack walked back to his pickup, pleased with the job John was doing. The younger man had worked for Jack part-time while attending college and helping to support a family of younger sisters and brothers, then worked his way up to foreman. Jack's confidence hadn't been misplaced. John Clearwater was intelligent, loyal and conscientious. If he said they needed more trucks, Jack could be sure it was true.

A popular love song began to play on the truck radio as he drove away from the site. Again his thoughts turned to Cassie. He could have found the time to call her, but he hadn't. Why was he playing these games with himself? He wanted to see her, but he'd put it off. Was he testing himself to see if he could keep away? The idea was an unsettling one, since she'd stayed firmly in his mind no matter what he did. Perhaps it was time to pay her a visit and see if the attraction he felt had begun to fade.

Cassie was dealing with one of the large sacks of ladybugs the pickers had left, and Blake was perched beside her, watching alertly for any beetles that might stray. He liked to play with them.

The front doorbell pealed, and Cassie grumbled under her breath while brushing off her hands. "Stay out of trouble," she told the cat before she went through the house to the front.

To her astonishment, Jack was standing on her porch holding a newspaper-wrapped package, his expression partially masked by mirrored sunglasses that reflected her own image. In faded jeans and a khaki shirt, two buttons open to expose a tuft of golden curls against his dark skin, he was devastating in an elementally male way. A baseball cap was pushed back on his head, and Cassie couldn't help but notice that it wasn't the one that had upset her before. This one sported the name of a popular brand of beer. Cassie brushed ineffectively at her own grubby cutoffs and stained tank top as Jack removed the sunglasses.

"Hello, Cass," he drawled in the deep voice that always made her mouth go dry.

"I wasn't expecting anyone," she said shortly, blocking the doorway as she reached for the scattered fragments of her composure.

Jack grinned, his gaze taking in her long, bare legs before returning slowly to her face. "Sorry to intrude," he murmured, his tone telling her he wasn't sorry at all. "I went fishing the other day, and I thought your cats might like the heads. I've been keeping them in the freezer."

Cassie paled and stared at the outstretched package, backing away a step. "H-heads?" she questioned. "Fish heads?"

He nodded. "For Blake and Crystal."

Belatedly remembering the manners her mother had drilled into her, Cassie stepped aside, glancing at the heavy, laced-up work boots that added another two inches to his already imposing height. "Come in," she offered. "I'm sure the cats, at least, will be glad to see you."

Jack winced at her less-than-enthusiastic welcome. "Thanks. Shall I put these right in the kitchen?"

"Why not?" Cassie trailed along behind him, trying not to notice how his big shoulders filled out the shirt, tapering to a slim waist and compact hips in the tight, worn jeans. He'd had time to go fishing but he hadn't had time to call her.

"I'm surprised to see you in broad daylight," she couldn't resist saying. He quirked an eyebrow, and she pointed next door. "Aren't you afraid your parents will know you're here?"

"It's Thursday," he replied, as if that explained everything. "Bingo."

Cassie nodded, understanding. Bingo at the local Eagles was a big draw on Thursday afternoons and Saturday evenings. She'd gone herself a few times when she had nothing better to do.

"No wonder you're so brave," she teased.

Jack set the package on the counter, then turned to reply to her gibes. Before he could speak, the phone rang.

Cassie answered, then listened to the familiar voice at the other end. "Hi, Mother," she said, her eyes shifting nervously to Jack as he waited by the sink. "What? No, you didn't interrupt anything." She lowered her voice, aware of his curious gaze.

As comprehension dawned, he tried to catch her eye, grinning and waggling his fingers. She turned away, hunching over the receiver.

"Of course I'm alone. Why would you think otherwise?"

Jack followed her in a complete circle as she kept turning, pointedly ignoring his smug face.

"Mother, I work during the day. I don't have time for rampant socializing."

"Can I say hello?" Jack hissed in a stage whisper.

Cassie moved as far away as the telephone cord would allow, her glare spitting darts. "Mother, I can't talk now. I see a delivery truck coming down the driveway."

There was a pause as Jack heard the faint sounds of her mother's voice at the other end.

"No, Mother," Cassie said on an exaggerated sigh. "It's not a florist truck."

After another brief exchange, she hung up the phone, red faced.

Jack's eyes were snapping with suppressed laughter. "Why didn't you want me to say hello?" he asked with feigned bewilderment. "Anyone would think you didn't want your mother to know you had a man standing in your kitchen." When Cassie gazed over his shoulder out the window and exhaled noisily, he continued, "I could have introduced myself—she knows my mom."

Cassie groaned and glared up at him. "You could do no such thing," she corrected him. "Do you know what you would be putting me through?"

Jack seemed to be deciding whether he was going to pursue the subject or let her off the hook as he wandered back toward the living room. Finally he paused at the front door. "Don't forget to put the fish in the fridge."

Cassie was relieved that he wasn't going to tease her further. "The least I can do is offer you a glass of juice since you were kind enough to bring over the, uh, parts."

"Got any beer?" Jack asked hopefully, turning toward her.

"No."

"Juice would be fine. It's not anything too way out, is it? Kiwifruit? Bell pepper?"

"Apple."

It wasn't until after Jack had downed the juice, given her a peck on the cheek and left without asking to see her again that Cassie remembered the package he'd brought. Back in the kitchen, she unwrapped it cautiously, wrinkling her nose at the odor as the two cats rubbed excitedly against her bare ankles and meowed loudly.

"Now isn't this interesting," Cassie muttered aloud as she studied the advertising printed on the inner wrapping.

Fred's Fish Market, it said in big red letters.

Chapter Five

Cassie was outside when the phone rang. She made a mad dash into the house, scattering cats as she went. Grabbing the receiver on the fourth ring, she gasped out a breathless hello.

"Sorry about that," said a familiar female voice. "Were you doing aerobics or weeding cauliflower?"

"Oh, hi, Bonnie. Actually I was picking caterpillars off the weeping plum tree."

"Ugh. I don't feel bad about taking you away from that."

Cassie chuckled. She and Bonnie Decker had met at a meeting of the organic gardening club several months before and had taken an instant liking to each other. Bonnie was a fiction writer, and also bred miniature dachshunds. She spent much of her spare time lobbying for stronger environmental laws.

"I'm calling about the new electronics plant that Japanese corporation is trying to push through down on Highway 50, on the way to Sacramento," Bonnie said.

"The one where they're planning on paving over the wetlands by Drury Creek?" The smile faded from Cassie's face. The project would wipe out several acres of marshy land that supported a thriving population of small animals and birds.

"The county wants a delay until a study can be made," Bonnie continued, "but I just heard today that there isn't any applicable law they can enforce."

Cassie leaped to her feet, pacing the kitchen with the receiver at her ear. "How can that be?"

"For some reason this project falls through the cracks. It's beginning to look like we'll have to do some heavy picketing, perhaps even more to drum up public awareness. Can we count you in?"

Cassie's hesitation took less than a heartbeat. "Sure," she said. "I just hope things don't get out of hand."

"They may, and we have to be prepared." Bonnie's voice was fierce with determination. "I'll keep you posted."

Cassie echoed her goodbye and hung up the phone. Chewing on her lip, she grabbed her gloves and went back outside. How could people be so irresponsible? For some reason Jack's smiling face popped into her head, and she frowned. Greed, that was the prime motivation.

Palmerton was a small town, named after Jonas and Wilma Palmerton, its first settlers. The area at its outskirts along Highway 50 toward Sacramento was being heavily developed, and the flavor of the town itself was gradually changing.

Cassie plunked two more fuzzy caterpillars into the metal container as her thoughts returned to Jack. She'd always known that someday her perfect mate would come along and the two of them would share interests, ideals and a basic reverence for the earth and its resources. Instead she found herself strongly attracted to a man who was arrogant, stubborn and uncaring about the issues closest to her heart. It was all so confusing, but Jack Hoffman was a hard man to dismiss.

Finished picking the voracious pests from the little plum tree, Cassie was about to go into her house when she heard a familiar laugh coming from next door. Glancing over at Mattie's backyard, she was startled to see the subject of her black thoughts standing on the redwood deck talking to his mother. He was wearing cutoffs and a tank top that did nothing to disguise the muscular strength of his shoulders and arms.

Mattie saw Cassie and waved. "Hello, dear. Isn't the heat something today?"

Cassie nodded and moved reluctantly to the fence separating the two properties. She noticed that Jack was trailing behind Mattie with equal hesitation, but there was a broad grin on his face that his mother couldn't see.

"You remember my son." Mattie smiled innocently. Behind his mother, Jack mugged outrageously, making Cassie flush with mingled annoyance and awareness of his powerful presence.

"Of course I do," she managed to say sweetly. "We did go out to dinner that time."

"Of course," Mattie agreed with a little chuckle, glancing over her shoulder.

Jack abruptly schooled his features, almost making Cassie burst out laughing.

Mattie turned back to Cassie. "Well, I have to have my hair done, so I'll leave you two. Jack is here to mow the lawn." When she stepped back from the fence she caught him looking at Cassie's legs.

"It's so warm, dear," she said in an even voice. "Feel free to leave the grass until it's cooler. There's fresh-baked brownies in the kitchen and lemonade in the fridge if you'd rather just—"

Jack rolled his eyes before cutting off Mattie's flow of words. "Thanks, Mom. You'd better hurry if you don't want to be late."

"Oh, yes." She shifted the straw purse on her arm to glance at her watch. "I'll be back later," she said to them both with a gleam in her eye that made Cassie want to squirm.

"See what I mean?" Jack demanded as they heard the sound of her car leaving. "She never quits."

"Just like my mother," Cassie agreed, stepping back.

"Where're you going?"

"Inside. I have paperwork to do." Cassie was secretly pleased to see a look of disappointment cross his masculine features. He might be dangerous and unsuitable, but he was still extremely attractive.

"Stay and talk a minute more," he requested, scratching his forearm.

"I see your rash isn't any better." Cassie noticed that, if anything, the red bumps had spread and intensified. "Have you put anything on it?"

"Some medicated cream, but it doesn't help much. It's got to be your cats that caused it. I can't think of anything else it could be."

Cassie snorted with disbelief. "I think you're ignoring the obvious," she retorted.

"It's not the pesticides," he said with a show of aggression.

She shrugged, unwilling to start an argument.

He leaned over the top of the fence, eyes intensely blue. "What we need to do," he said in a much gentler voice, "is to spend some time together at my apartment where there aren't any fuzzy little critters to make me break out."

"What, no dust bunnies under the tables?" she asked.

"No what?"

"Dust bunnies. Those balls of dust that appear when you don't vacuum. I thought all bachelors had them."

"Not if they have a Mrs. Cameron," he retorted, "like I do."

"What's a Mrs. Cameron?"

"A proper, English, cleaning lady. The dust bunnies wouldn't *dare* hang around when Mrs. Cameron arrives with her mops and her brooms." He twisted the end of his mustache and wiggled his eyebrows villainously.

"You're spoiled." Cassie felt a twinge of envy. She hated housework.

Jack was more interested in whether Cassie would consider his invitation than in discussing domestic help. Her sometimes prickly, always unpredictable nature intrigued him, just as her long, slim legs attracted him. He would love to get her alone at his apartment, even if it was just to talk and swim in the pool without worrying that his nosy mother would find out.

"We could take a dip and then barbecue some dinner," he added. "There's hardly ever many people in the pool, and the deck off my apartment is cool and shady in the evening." He leaned closer and his voice softened. "How about tomorrow night?"

A parade of emotions crossed Cassie's face, easy for him to decipher. Interest was followed by caution, reluctant curiosity and then grudging resignation. The last was hardly flattering to his male ego.

"Six o'clock?" he pushed, not waiting for her agreement. When she didn't answer immediately, he glanced past her to the large, meticulously maintained garden. "You could bring a salad. I haven't eaten anything green and healthy for a week."

"Oh, all right," she agreed as enthusiastically as if she was making an appointment to have her teeth cleaned. "Tomorrow night would be fine. No need for you to come over the back fence this time, just give me directions."

Her eyes began to sparkle with a mischievous light that Jack chose to ignore. "I'll pick you up," he said, not bothering to add that his parents would be at his sister's.

Cassie's eyes widened innocently, but her tone was mocking. "It must be the heat," she murmured. "See you at six."

Jack was too happy that she had accepted to answer her barb. Instead he turned away to start on the lawn. He still had to do a job for Sierra and then meet his foreman for a progress report before he was done for the day.

When she went into the house, Cassie called her brother, Tom, at his shop to see if he could come by for supper that evening. She wasn't sure if she wanted to tell him about Jack or not, but the thought of Tom's undemanding company was an appealing one. Unfortunately he was in the middle of airbrushing a custom design on a new Trans AM for some game show host from Burbank, and couldn't come to the phone. Leaving a message, she went back to work.

When Jack woke the next morning his arms were bright red and itchy, too itchy to delay a visit to the doctor even one more day.

"A friend of mine has two cats," he began when Dr. Roberts studied the rash on his forearms, his voice trailing off when the doctor started to shake his head.

"I've seen this before, and I'd say it was something else." Dr. Roberts examined the skin closer. "What line of work are you in?"

Fifteen minutes later Jack was on his way to the adjoining pharmacy with a written prescription, and with the doctor's words ringing in his ears. Repeated exposure to the ingredients contained in Raydelon II, which the doctor had looked up, could cause skin irritation, dizziness, asthmalike symptoms and even brain damage in a small number of susceptible humans.

Jack was stunned. Cassie had been right, and he had been *wrong, wrong, wrong.* When he climbed back into his truck with the prescription in a sack, he wrapped his fingers around the steering wheel and stared hard at a pregnant woman who was walking by with a small child in tow. Snarling a sudden, violent oath, Jack smacked the flat of his hand against the wheel. He knew what he had to do.

The next evening Cassie was putting the final touches on her salad, an attractive, layered creation in a glass bowl, when the doorbell rang. Tom had had other plans the evening before, and she'd spent most of today packing ladybugs and taking them to the post office. By the time six o'clock rolled around, Cassie was more than a little tired of her own company.

As usual, at the sound of the bell, Blake darted to safety and Crystal headed for the front door, growling low in her throat.

"Down, girl," Cassie told the bristling cat, brushing by. "It's Jack."

As if she recognized the name, Crystal leaped to the back of a chair and began washing her front paws, totally relaxed as Cassie opened the door.

"Hi. Are you ready?" Jack's smile was warm, his gaze approving as he glanced at her white terry jumpsuit, belted at the waist with a multicolored woven tie that matched the straps of her Mexican huarache sandals. Tiny straw sombreros dangled from her ears.

"It would have made more sense for me to drive myself," Cassie said as she stepped aside and he walked through the door.

"Why? Afraid you'd be leaving suddenly?" he asked, tipping his head to the side to study her more closely. "I promise I won't pounce on you until *after* dinner."

Cassie stared, not altogether sure if he was teasing until he gave her an exaggerated up and down perusal, smacking his lips and rubbing his palms together. Reluctantly she smiled at his expression. Perhaps it was herself she needed to worry about the most. He drew her like a bumblebee to purple clover, and she seemed unable to resist him. The way her nostrils flared to drink in the mingled scents of soap and musk that wafted her way like beckoning fingers proved it, and her repeated reminders to herself that he was a money-grubbing capitalist with no conscience didn't help at all.

"Just a sec," she said, ignoring his last remark. In the kitchen, she covered the salad bowl with plastic wrap and slipped it and a container of homemade herb dressing into a paper bag. Earlier she'd stuffed the only one-piece swimsuit she owned and a few other necessities into a large purse, which she picked up on her way back through the living room.

Sometime later when Cassie walked out of Jack's guest bedroom wearing the suit, he studied her for a long moment without speaking. Cassie might have remembered to be embarrassed if she wasn't equally busy looking at him.

The image of male perfection he presented in the brief trunks should have been no surprise after the numerous, tantalizing glimpses she'd already had. Still, the sight of all that tanned skin and rippling muscle at once was a bit overwhelming, she thought dazedly, picking up a towel and managing to partially shield herself with it as she walked toward the sliding door.

"Shall we go?" she asked, gratified that her voice sounded normal.

His grin was wry. "We'd better," he muttered. "I need some cooling off."

The heat spread over Cassie's cheeks like an oil spill on ocean waters as she preceded him down the path to the pool, feeling the force of his gaze boring into her back. He'd showed her the blue expanse when they first arrived, and she had been pleasantly surprised.

No rectangular pit in a frame of concrete aggregate, the pool was instead a free-form jewel set attractively into a landscaped frame. The surrounding gardens provided several places to sit and relax if tenants grew bored with their own decks, which were all screened for privacy. She'd been even more surprised and impressed to hear that the whole complex had been one of Jack's projects.

Now he pulled two chaise longues together and yanked the towel from around his neck. "Are you a leaper or an incher?" he asked.

Cassie's face screwed itself into a perplexed frown. "A what or a what?"

"Do you jump right in or proceed by inches, first the big toe..." His gaze meandered up her leg, hesitated fractionally at her breasts, and eventually found its way to her face.

Cassie hadn't blushed so much since the first time she'd driven her unusually painted car. Instead of answering his question, she dropped her towel onto the closest chaise longue and dove into the dazzling blue water.

When she surfaced Jack was swimming next to her, gleaming droplets shining like gems against his dark skin. For almost an hour they raced and played, having the large pool to themselves.

Cassie was a good swimmer, that being one of a score of lessons she had taken as a child. Jack, however, had the power and grace of a natural athlete. The races that she did manage to win, Cassie had a sneaking suspicion he'd let her.

Another couple came to the pool, and Jack called a greeting. They waved back from the other side, then two more men came down. One was carrying a large beach ball and the other had a portable tape player he proceeded to tune in to a soft-rock station.

"Are you getting hungry," Jack asked Cassie, "or would you rather stay a little longer?"

"I'm starved."

He nodded before climbing out and offering her a hand. When Cassie was beside him, he picked up her towel and began to pat her dripping hair.

"I can do that," she protested.

He let the towel slide around her shoulders and pulled her lightly forward. Before she could protest, he dropped a brief kiss on her wet lips. His mouth was firm and slightly cool, and Cassie barely caught herself from swaying toward him. With a devilish grin, he released the towel and took her hand.

"Come on," he said. "I've got some beautiful steaks, and I can't wait to try your salad."

"Especially since you haven't eaten anything green and healthy in so long," she reminded him dryly.

For a moment he looked blank, then he grinned rather sheepishly. "Right."

From the shape of his nearly perfect body, Cassie suspected he must watch what he ate more closely than he would admit. It took more than just fantastic genes to maintain a specimen like Jack Hoffman.

Back on his outside deck, he lighted the charcoal while Cassie changed, then she admired the thick fillets he'd set out.

"I make my own barbecue sauce," he said, oiling the grill. "If you like it I might be persuaded to share my secret recipe."

"It would have to be exceptional to top the marinade I use," Cassie retorted. "Can I help with anything?"

"You could set the table while I change. Everything's in there." He pointed vaguely toward the gleaming oak cupboards above the tiled kitchen counter. "We'll just pop the spuds in the microwave when the meat's about ready."

While he was gone, Cassie took a few minutes to explore the spotless kitchen that opened onto the deck. The apartment was a two-story town house, elegantly furnished in pale colors and modern lines. She couldn't help thinking, as she wandered back through the austere living room, how much warmer it would look with a few touches from her own home. An afghan thrown across the back of the cream linen couch, bouquets of dried weeds on the glass-topped tables, a couple of pillows to add color to the love seat.

Cassie caught herself just in time, returning to the kitchen to root around for plates and silverware. There was no point in thinking how their possessions could complement each other any more than trying to mesh their divergent personalities. They were too different.

Once they were seated over dinner, Jack hitched up his chair, determined to tell Cassie about his decision to disband Sierra Pest Control, after all. The cream he'd gotten from the doctor had already started to work; the only thing left of the rash was an expanse of bumps, but the redness was almost completely gone.

Jack had no intention of admitting that Cassie had been right about the chemicals. He was still shocked by the doctor's words, feeling naive and neglectful for being involved in something without first checking it out thoroughly. No way would he have used building materials without making sure they were safe and reliable, but that was exactly what he'd done in spraying pesticides all over the place. He wasn't ready to hear Cassie's condemnations heaped on top of his own.

He speared a bite of the tender steak, glaring at it with displeasure.

"Is yours tough?" Cassie asked, misinterpreting his frown. "Mine's divine."

He shifted his gaze from the offending bite of meat to her big brown eyes. "I'm disbanding Sierra," he said shortly, setting down his fork.

An excited grin transformed Cassie's face at his words, making him feel like a heel for not being willing to admit the truth.

"My accountant thinks it would be a good tax break," he rushed on before she could question him.

Cassie frowned, not understanding. How could closing down a business be beneficial? She knew enough about bookkeeping to get by, but the finer points of creative accounting were beyond her comprehension. "What about the employees?" she asked.

"Juan's coming to work at Hoffman Construction, and Donna, the secretary, is going on maternity leave. I'll find her something when she comes back."

He looked away, as if the admiration in Cassie's eyes embarrassed him.

"I think that's wonderful," she said finally, not quite accepting his explanation about a tax advantage. She didn't know why he might not be telling her the whole story, but it was too nice an evening to push it. Perhaps he would elaborate later.

When they'd finished eating and had cleared up the dishes, twilight had settled in around them. They sat on deck chairs in companionable silence, drinking sangria and listening to the strains of guitar music from a nearby balcony.

Cassie would have liked to reopen the topic and question Jack further, but she sensed a reluctance in him. "I see your rash is better," she commented instead.

He glanced down at his forearms almost furtively. "Uh, yeah. I told you we should come here."

Cassie smiled her agreement. "Anything to help the suffering," she murmured, slightly puzzled. Perhaps it had been something he'd eaten.

"This is nice," she murmured when he remained silent. "I thought a big complex like this would be noisy, but it's not."

"Even though the building's one of my own, it's only temporary lodging for me," Jack said. "I'd like to build a house someday, but it has to have the right feel to it, not too modern." He took a sip from his glass. "Cozy, like your house," he added.

"Mine?" Cassie was surprised. From the stark way Jack's apartment was decorated, she pictured him as the brass-and-glass type, with no room for the dried flowers and homey touches she'd want to add.

He turned to her in the gathering darkness. "Yes," he continued. "Your house feels like a home, not something out of a decorating magazine. At the risk of sounding silly, I'd say it has soul." His gaze shifted away as if the admission had embarrassed him.

"More like that lived-in look," Cassie said dryly. She knew that some of her furniture was worn and that her living room rug needed replacing. The kitchen was roomy but old-fashioned and there wasn't enough closet space.

Jack looked at her. "I don't mean the worn spot in the front carpet or the way the couch sags," he said earnestly, proving he'd really looked around. "I mean your handmade touches. I assume you did them, or at least picked them out. The yarn plant hangers, the pillows, that bowl of dried leaves."

"Those are weeds," Cassie corrected him.

"Yeah, weeds," he agreed. "But they still add to the overall appearance." He stopped and sighed, obviously exasperated.

"I think I know what you mean. You could do the same thing here if you wanted to. A few flowers, a couple of bright pillows, some pictures..." Her voice trailed off as he shook his head.

"This is temporary," he repeated. "The furniture's leased. There's time for the other stuff when I have a place of my own."

Cassie nodded. She understood, and this new facet to his personality surprised her. Had she assumed that because Jack's values were different from hers that he had no depth? Perhaps she'd been hasty.

A light breeze sprang up, and she shivered.

Jack immediately leaped to his feet. "You're cold. Shall we go in?"

Cassie shook her head. The guitar music had stopped, but she had no wish to go back into the silent, private apartment. It was too tempting.

"I'll get you a wrap." He slipped through the slider before Cassie had a chance to protest. In minutes she heard the strains of a Gary Morris tape coming from the living room, then Jack returned with a long-sleeved chambray shirt.

"This do?" he said. "I didn't think it was cool enough for a sweater."

Cassie nodded, standing to slip her bare arms into its voluminous sleeves. Jack rolled the cuffs back several times, then straightened the collar. Trying not to be obvious, she sniffed at the fabric to see if it carried his scent, but the only thing she smelled was the faint tang of lemon laundry soap.

"Dance?" he asked, holding out his arms.

"Out here?" Cassie remembered how sweet dancing with Jack could be. When he nodded and urged her to come closer, she stepped into his embrace, extremely conscious of his unbuttoned shirt and the animal heat radiating from his body like the rays of a second sun.

Dancing on the deck was really little more than swaying and shuffling their feet, but to Jack it was an excuse to hold Cassie, something he'd been thinking about all day. He rubbed his cheek against her hair and tucked their entwined hands between them. Her nails grazed his bare chest, causing a ripple of awareness to shiver over his sensitized skin. The fingers of his other hand spread wide on her back, as if memorizing the delicate feel of her while he absorbed the caress of her light breath against the skin of his throat.

When the song ended, Cassie made a move to step away, but Jack's arm tightened and his free hand skated along her jaw, stopping to tilt up her chin. In the light from the window he studied her face. Dark, mysterious eyes stared back at him, framed by curling lashes. Her full, lush lips parted as his gaze touched them. Swallowing, he bent his head.

Cassie reached around his neck as his mouth descended. In the dim light the expression in his narrowed eyes was impossible to read, but his mouth was softly curved and infinitely tempting.

After the first gentle press of lips, he broke the subtle contact, then touched her mouth with the very tip of his tongue, slowly outlining its edges and teasing its corners.

Cassie's lips parted on a sigh, and he slipped inside, caressing, stroking. His mustache was a tactile stimulant, tickling the sensitive skin of her upper lip, adding its own unique stamp to the kiss.

When Cassie moaned and leaned closer, Jack's arms tightened and his lips became more aggressive, less tentative. His hands stroked her back, her waist, her hips as his mouth explored hers with a bold insistence that took her breath away.

For a moment Cassie answered kiss for kiss, caress for caress as her fingers skimmed lightly down his bare chest, feeling the ripple her touch caused to dance across his skin. She tangled her tongue with his, enjoying the rough-smooth textures of his mouth.

Jack broke the kiss to murmur something dark and rich, something unintelligible. Then he buried his lips in the hollow of her throat as his big hand caressed the rounded curve of her bottom, pulling her intimately close. As his body pressed against her, reason struggled to return and she placed her open palms on his chest, feeling its shallow rise and fall.

"Jack," she murmured, then again when he didn't respond.

He stilled and his touch became gentler.

"Yes, baby, what is it?" His voice was deep, thicker.

She pulled out of his arms, straightening the borrowed shirt that had become bunched between them. "I think it's time to take me home," she said, eyes lowered.

What would he think of her sudden halt to what was quickly blazing out of control? Would he be angry, impatient, sarcastic after she'd participated in the heated embrace so willingly? Other men had reacted in all those ways after less passionate kisses, assuming she would be eager to share more intimate exchanges.

Jack leaned down, touching his forehead to hers as he pulled a long, shaking breath into what sounded like tortured lungs.

"I guess you're right," he agreed after a pause, voice not quite steady. "But, God, I hate to let you go." For emphasis he pulled her hips sharply to his, then almost instantly dropped his hands.

Cassie was having a great deal of trouble with her own breathing. She'd never before felt the strong desire that was throbbing through her now. Finally she understood why her friends sometimes had such a difficult job saying no, why they didn't always succeed. Before she'd thought it was a simple decision; now she realized that passion could be an overwhelming force—one that could sweep her away.

With shaking hands she pushed her hair back and slipped off the borrowed shirt as Jack opened the sliding door to the apartment.

They were silent during the ride back, but it was a pleasant silence, one Cassie had no wish to disturb. This time she'd chosen the middle seat belt on the wide bench of his truck, and he'd placed one of her hands on his thigh before returning both of his to the steering wheel. Soft music played on the tape deck as they rode through the evening darkness.

"I'd like to see where you work sometime," Jack said suddenly, piercing the quiet. "Perhaps I could come over when you're doing whatever it is you do to those little red bugs." He glanced at her questioningly before turning back to the road ahead.

"Sure," Cassie agreed, startled by his interest. "I'm expecting another delivery in a couple of days."

"You work on the weekends?"

"Don't you if the job requires it?"

"Well, sure," he drawled. "Can't hold up a construction crew if you get behind because of the weather or a delayed shipment."

"Same here," she said, feeling slightly defensive. "The aphids won't wait."

"I s'pose not." His tone was doubtful. "Would you give me a call when it's convenient?"

"Okay." Her response was slow. She was only getting in deeper, she realized as he sent her a crinkling smile. Then a little jolt of happiness forked through her at the prospect of knowing she'd be seeing him again soon, and she forgot all about the reasons it could never work between them.

Chapter Six

Sorry I couldn't make it the other night."

The sound of Tom's deep voice on the phone made Cassie smile. Her brother was four years older, and they'd spent most of their growing-up years teasing and tormenting each other. Still, he'd always been there when she needed him, and they'd stayed very close.

"There was this fabulous redhead who came in to have her car fixed—"

"I should have known," she interrupted. "How do you do it?" Tom's success with women didn't surprise her; he was good-looking and had a terrific personality. What did continue to amaze her was his total lack of awareness of both his popularity and its reasons.

"We had a date the night you invited me over," he continued, ignoring her interruption. "But it turned out that Candy had read about the car I customized for Brandon Reno, the singer. All she wanted to hear about was which celebrities I've met."

His voice had an edge of disappointment. Cassie knew it bothered him when people were only interested in his success and not in Tom Culpepper, the person. He could open a custom car business in L.A. and get rich; instead he chose to stay in Palmerton and let the celebrities come to him.

"Sorry, babe," she said. "Not every woman is like that. And we'll have to make dinner another time."

"Yeah. What's new in your life?"

Instantly she thought of Jack. "Nothing much."

"All that hard work you're always doing will make you dull," Tom teased. Instead of keeping long hours and expanding his business, Tom turned down as many jobs as he accepted and took plenty of time off to pursue his other interests.

"How about going waterskiing with me next week? Denny's going to run his new boat on Lake Tahoe."

"Wouldn't you rather take a girl?" Cassie asked.

"You're a girl."

"You know what I mean, a date."

"Uh, can't think of anyone, unless you wanted to bring somebody yourself."

Cassie thought again of Jack with a twinge of regret. In a way she would like him and Tom to meet, but she was still too unsure of Jack and of her own feelings. If Tom suspected her interest in Jack, he would ask questions she couldn't answer. With an effort, she switched her thoughts to the legion of local women who'd kill for a date with her tall, brown-eyed brother. "There's no one special I can think of to bring," she said. "Keep me posted, okay?"

They lingered on the phone for a few more moments and then Cassie said goodbye. She couldn't help but wonder how much longer her brother would manage to avoid the net. Between their mother's matchmaking and the determination of several of Cassie's friends, he was definitely an endangered species.

She'd barely set the phone down when it rang again.

"I hope you're not busy," Bonnie said breathlessly. "I've been trying to get through to you."

"What's up?" It took a lot to ruffle Bonnie's usual calm.

"We're picketing at the job site for the electronics plant this afternoon," her friend said, "and Channel 3 has promised to send someone out. We heard that ground breaking is next week, and we've just got to stop it. Can you come today?"

Cassie hesitated. She had tomatoes to pick and her column to outline. "What time?" she asked. Perhaps the demonstration would give her something to write about.

"One-thirty, and I can pick you up. Wait'll you see the great picket signs I made."

Cassie glanced at the butterfly wall clock and agreed. She'd have just enough time to get the tomatoes picked and delivered before Bonnie got there.

After lunching with Sam Okimoto, the representative from the company that was responsible for his next building project, Jack drove the older man out to the section of land they'd soon be clearing. There was a roll of plans and blueprints behind the seat in Jack's truck that the two men had spent the morning studying, but they both wanted to see the actual site again.

Jack knew that a large amount of his time would be spent at this location during the next few months, and he was glad that the pest control business had been taken care of. He'd sold off the tank trucks to a heating oil firm, and leased the property to a health food chain. The rash on his arms was gone and his conscience was clear.

"What the hell's that?" Sam was pointing at a group of people carrying signs and blocking the dirt road onto the property. The crowd of about twenty picketers parted reluctantly as Jack slowed the truck, driving past them with care.

Just what he and the Yano Corporation needed, more bad publicity, he thought with a grimace as he noticed a car bearing the insignia of a local television station. Sam had told him earlier that his office received several crank letters after the newspaper story about the new plant appeared. Now two people with a microphone and camera were interviewing one of the protestors. As Jack swept the truck into a U-turn, the reporter turned in their direction.

Sam groaned. "I don't want to tango with that barracuda today. She thinks that 'go for the ratings' and 'go for the jugular vein' mean the same thing." He slapped his hand against his knee. "Doesn't anyone care that we're bringing in hundreds of pollution-free jobs?" Frustration was evident in his usually well-modulated voice.

"A lot of people care, and they're eager to have a branch of your company as a neighbor." Jack tried to placate the other man as they headed back through the throng. "It's only a few idiots..." His voice trailed off as he noticed a familiar face in the crowd advancing on the truck.

Damn, he hadn't expected to see Cassie among the angry citizens, but on second thought her presence didn't surprise him. They seemed destined to be at opposite ends of every issue that came up.

Blue eyes clashed with brown before Jack's attention was jerked away by the thud of a wooden sign handle against the fender of his truck. "Hey!" He wasn't sure who'd done it, but the aggressive act surprised him. These people were serious. And hostile.

For a second he pictured the architect's rendering of the red brick buildings and carefully landscaped grounds that would take the place of empty fields and swampland. Then he muttered a curse under his breath and accelerated past the crowd, ignoring the cloud of dust his tires raised and the insistent shouts of the reporter from Channel 3. Beside him, Sam Okimoto sat rigidly, eyes front as a last picketer banged a fist against his closed window.

"I'll have to prepare a statement and call the station," Sam said, his voice once again calm. "If you'd take me back to my car, I'd appreciate it."

Jack glanced at the other man's grave expression. "No problem." His mind began to work through the new situation he'd have to deal with. It could get awfully sticky if the picketers planned to keep the protest going while his men were trying to work, not to mention the danger to both groups.

He planned to call his lawyer right away to see what they could do to stop the protestors before the actual work started and someone got hurt. Then he'd have to talk to Cassie. His attempts to shove her from his mind had been as successful as stopping a flow of wet cement with his bare hands, but this new development might really spell the end for them.

Cassie was hot, sweaty and angry when Bonnie dropped her off an hour later. "I should have known," she grumbled to Crystal as the cat rubbed against her ankle. "Where there's pollution and environmental murder, you'll find Jack Hoffman smack in the middle of it. The man's a menace!"

Crystal gazed up at her with sapphire-blue eyes and purred loudly.

After a quick shower, she was toweling her hair when the doorbell rang. Straightening the faded Bruce is the Boss, but Neil's a Diamond T-shirt she'd pulled on over worn cutoffs, she yanked open the front door, still steaming from the shock of seeing Jack at the protest site.

"Hi." The object of her anger was leaning against the door frame, his expression almost as grim as her own.

Cassie attempted to shut the door in his face, but before she could he shoved a booted foot in the way.

"We need to talk," he said, pushing past her.

Irrelevantly, Cassie's hand went to her tangled, wet hair. She must look a mess. Then annoyance at his high-handed attitude took over.

"Just a minute—" she sputtered, following him into the living room. "You can't just burst—"

"I *said* we need to talk." His tone was dark and threatening, and his eyes were shooting sparks.

For a moment Cassie faltered as if she were the one in the wrong. Then she moved forward aggressively, tripped over the cat and all but fell into Jack's waiting arms.

Without thinking, he caught her to him. Her feminine curves pressed against his chest and her fingers curled around the muscles of his upper arms. He sucked in a lungful of her scented shampoo along with the clean, wet smell of her hair as he dragged her even closer. For a moment his lips touched her temple as she relaxed against his length, and his pulses quickened. Then she stiffened, her hands beginning to push at his chest.

"What do you think you're doing?" she demanded, pulling back. "You can't just barge in here—"

"You're the one who threw yourself at me," Jack couldn't resist pointing out.

"I tripped." Her voice was icy.

"Oh, hell," Jack growled. She was mad anyway, might as well be hanged for a horse thief as not. He jerked her back into his embrace. "Shut up."

Cassie's eyes widened at his clipped command, and her jaw dropped. Her parted lips were all the encouragement he needed. Jack bent his head and captured her mouth with his, forgetting for one blissful moment everything that had come between them.

On a moan of frustration, Cassie gave in, splaying her hands across his wide back and returning his kiss with enthusiasm. The second he felt her response, Jack gentled the hard pressure of his mouth, sliding his hands from her shoulders to her hips and back, gathering her close.

After a timeless moment, he lifted his lips from hers and stared into her brown eyes.

"Cassie..."

A burning pain exploded against his shin and he howled in surprise and anguish.

"You kicked me!" He couldn't believe she could change so quickly—from liquid fire in his arms to a hothead who tried to break his leg.

She wiped her mouth with the back of her hand while Jack rubbed furiously at the aching spot on his shin.

"Get out of here, you, you, *despoiler*!" Cassie's fists were jammed against her hips, and she was glaring as if he'd just slithered out from under a rock.

It was Jack's turn to gape openmouthed. "Despoiler? Because I'm helping to bring hundreds of jobs to our community? Lady, have you read the unemployment rates lately?'' he shouted, trying to ignore the dull throb in his leg. "You should be thanking me!"

Cassie stuck out her chin. "Men like you would pave over the Grand Canyon," she retorted. "You have no *soul*!"

Jack was keenly aware that once again he was failing to follow the direction of her argument. Perhaps she really was mentally unhinged, after all.

He remembered the way she'd just kissed him and decided to give her the benefit of the doubt.

"Can't we discuss this sensibly?" he asked, wincing as he shifted his weight to his injured leg. Already the bruise felt like a goose egg. Then he glanced down at her tennis shoe. Perhaps it wouldn't be quite that bad.

Before him, Cassie sucked in a long, quivering breath. She eyed the khaki work shirt that strained across his wide shoulders and the matching pants that hugged his muscular thighs. The tan fabric made his blond hair look like raw, golden silk and intensified the blue of his eyes.

She was keenly aware of the hunger his body had aroused when he'd pressed against her, but she realized also that her feelings toward Jack were more complex than a mere physical yearning. Somewhere along the line her emotions had also become involved.

"Okay," she agreed, telling herself it was only fair to listen to him. She plopped down into the bentwood rocker and indicated the couch with her hand before folding her arms across her chest. "So talk."

Instead of sitting down, Jack walked over to where Blake was perched on the back of a recliner, and scratched the cat's ears. A faint rumbling began in Blake's chest, and he pushed his head into Jack's hand.

Cassie stared straight ahead. After a moment, Jack sighed and dropped to the couch. "This is an important project to me," he began. Cassie's frown told him that he'd started from the wrong angle.

He began again. "The Yano Corporation has a reputation for responsibility to its employees and to its community—they'll be a good neighbor." He realized that his words sounded like a well-rehearsed sales pitch.

While he was speaking, Cassie studied his face intently. "That's not the point," she said heatedly. "The animals who are losing their homes don't care if Yano is a good employer."

Jack frowned at her sarcastic tone. This discussion was going nowhere. Perhaps this wasn't the time to try to convince her of his sincerity.

"What are your friends' plans?" he asked, changing tactics abruptly. "How much interference are they going to make?"

Cassie looked scandalized. "I can't tell you that! You're on the other side, and I'm no spy." Briefly she wondered what Bonnie and the others would think if they knew the head of Hoffman Construction was in her living room, sprawled on her couch.

"Just don't get in the way of one of my bulldozers," Jack muttered half under his breath, getting up. He raked a hand through his hair, frustration evident in his narrow-eyed gaze.

Cassie rose, too. "Are you going to run over me if I do?" she demanded.

A reluctant grin tugged at Jack's mouth. He knew they were both getting ridiculous. "How can you respond to me one minute—" his gaze swept the length of her and back "—then hint that I might turn you into part of the parking lot the next?" He forced a teasing note into his voice, despite the lingering ache in his leg. "Not to mention your attempt to cripple me."

His eyes held a hint of unwilling humor as Cassie faced him. Realizing there was probably no way either of them could swing the other's opinion, she took a deep breath and managed to relax. She'd just have to think of some other way to help stop the project. It was easy to see that Jack had no intentions of abandoning it.

"Since you're here, would you like to see my mail order business?" she asked, determined to change the subject and keep him around for a few moments longer. The desire to get rid of him had fled somewhere between their kiss and the warmth of his smile.

"You mean the bugs? Sure." If Cassie was going to extend an olive branch, he intended to grab it. Perhaps she would understand the importance of this new project to the area after she'd thought about it for a while. It would be nice if she did, but he had little hope that she'd change her mind.

"Come on, then. I'll take you on the ten-cent tour of my converted garage."

"Sounds a little weird," he couldn't help but comment as he followed her through the house.

Stepping into the large workroom, he was surprised at the efficient way everything was set up. In his mind he'd been picturing some little cottage industry she dabbled in when she wasn't out tilting at windmills. There were four old white refrigerators lined up against the walls and a neatly folded stack of cloth sacks by several pieces of equipment he couldn't identify. The whole area was scrupulously clean.

Cassie opened the door of one fridge, revealing rows of cardboard containers.

"Looks like Chinese take-out," Jack commented as he stared inside. "Is that where you keep the bugs?"

He was only kidding, and it surprised him when Cassie nodded.

"They're hibernating."

He looked at her sharply to see if she was pulling his leg. "Like bears?"

"I'm serious. Below a certain temperature they go dormant. They can live for three to four months in that state, but usually I ship them out in a matter of days."

"Where do you get them?" he asked. "Do you breed them yourself?" He hadn't seen anything that looked like ladybug nurseries in the big room.

"No, I pay people to harvest them. The pickers claim certain beds where the ladybugs cluster during their migration into the Sierra foothills. Vacuum cleaners powered by small generators are used to gather the ladybugs, or they're just shoveled, dirt and all, into the cloth bags. We sort them with this big shaker." She pointed to the strange piece of equipment Jack had noticed earlier.

"Then I put them into cold storage. When it's time to ship them, we spray them with water to give them a drink, and sort them again so we're only shipping live bugs."

She moved around to a second fridge and opened the door, studying the piles of full cloth bags before shutting it again. "We ship March to May, then in June we harvest what we call the second cycle—the newly hatched one we send out until fall."

Jack shook his head. "This is quite a procedure. You don't ship all year?"

"No, the bugs go dormant when the snow is on the ground. In the spring they go down to Yosemite to feed, then return to the beds in the Sierras to lay eggs. When they hatch it makes up the second cycle I mentioned."

Jack looked around the tidy work area. "Where do you get your mailing list?" he asked, the business part of his brain ticking away.

Cassie leaned a slim hip against a battered table. "I advertise in several gardening magazines, and people just send in orders."

Jack was getting excited as he thought of the ways she could expand what looked like a small operation.

"You should keep a list of interested people on your computer, send them out a flyer a couple of times a year to remind them that you're here." He began to pace as ideas came to him. "You could buy mailing lists, too. There are places that sell specialized ones."

Cassie was frowning but he assumed she was thinking about what he'd said.

"Is there a limit to the supply of ladybugs you can get?" he asked.

She shook her head. "But—"

He held up a detaining hand. "I'm sure there are a lot of creative ways to advertise," he said enthusiastically. "You've probably barely tapped the market."

"Jack . . ."

"You could sell more ads, maybe get a plug on some local gardening shows up and down the coast." He could see her business outgrowing the garage.

"Jack!"

He glanced at Cassie, surprised to see her in the stance that was becoming all too familiar: balled fists on hips, chin stuck out. He stopped pacing.

"Huh?"

"My business is doing just fine." Her tone was level, patient.

"Yeah, but this is small potatoes compared to what you could do."

"I *like* small potatoes." Her voice changed as if she were speaking through clenched teeth.

Jack looked closely, his enthusiasm draining away when he saw that her dark eyes were fairly snapping with anger. Something told him that the bloom on her cheeks wasn't put there by any appreciation of his presence, and she was tapping one small foot.

"I was just trying to help," he said in a subdued voice.

"I don't need your help. I have no wish to blanket the United States with ladybugs." Her voice rose. "I am doing *just fine* with my small potatoes."

The way she emphasized the last two words made him wince. Had he said that?

She led the way through the kitchen, her back ramrod straight. Even her hair seemed to be quivering.

As Jack followed her through the house, Cassie tried to get a grip on her temper. Trust him to ignore what she'd accomplished, instead bombarding her with suggestions she didn't appreciate. No, not suggestions but arrogant commands that she expand. No wonder the man built huge manufacturing plants and condo complexes. He probably lived by the motto Bigger is Better.

"I have a lot to do," she said, holding open the front door. "Thanks for stopping by."

Jack looked as if he was going to say something. Instead his mouth thinned, and his blue eyes began to glitter. Cassie was sure that the color creeping up his neck had nothing to do with sunburn.

"I have to be going anyway," he said. "I have, uh, plans for this evening." His gaze didn't quite meet hers.

A prick of pain hit Cassie like the sting of a hornet at his words, then she remembered what had brought him to her house in the first place. "Me, too. I have plans, too," she said, unable to control her tongue. "See you at the picket line."

Jack started to turn after he'd stepped onto the porch, but Cassie hastily shut the door. Moments later she heard the roar of his truck engine. If Mattie missed his departure she needed a hearing aid.

Cassie's plans for the evening consisted of watching an old movie of Charlton Heston being promoted from galley slave to chariot driver, while her cats both tried to squeeze onto her lap at the same time. During the commercials she thought about Jack and the hole his departure would leave in her life. After today she was certain he wouldn't be around again. Convincing herself she was glad took more effort than she wanted to expend at the time. Instead she carried on a running conversation with the cats, muttering that at least the ancient Romans hadn't gone around polluting the environment—they were too busy feeding people to the lions.

Cassie had just finished trimming the edges of her lawn with the Weed Eater a few days later when Mattie came to the fence that divided their properties.

"Do you have time for a break and a glass of lemonade?" she asked.

Cassie had been beginning to feel vaguely guilty for ducking into the house whenever she saw her neighbor. Deciding that she couldn't spend the rest of her life pretending Jack's mother didn't live next door, she brushed off her hands and smiled.

"Lemonade sounds wonderful."

Moments later they were seated on the Hoffman's deck holding tall glasses of the tart liquid and idly discussing the record-breaking heat wave.

"How's Karen and her family?" Cassie asked when the conversation lulled. She had taken an instant liking to Jack's sister.

"They're all fine. Karen loves her children and Ben so much. She told me just the other day how much more fulfilling her life has been since she got married and had her family."

Cassie smiled weakly. Mattie was as subtle as her own mother, who had called an hour before. As subtle as a wrecking ball kissing the side of a condemned building.

"I'm happy for her," she said, reaching for an oat-meal cookie that she really didn't want.

Mattie hesitated, then cleared her throat. "You and Jack have a spat?" she finally asked. "I thought I heard his truck the other afternoon."

"Haven't you talked to him?" It had been almost a week; surely Mattie had already heard Jack's version of his failed attempts to restructure her life.

Mattie shook her head. "He's so busy with some new project, the biggest his company has ever handled." Her face was flushed with motherly pride. "He said that this job will ensure his success. The Japanese company that's locating here is into all kinds of projects, and if he does well, he'll have an inside track with them."

Cassie almost choked on her lemonade. When she'd recovered, she was tempted to enlighten Mattie as to what Jack was really up to with his project, but one more look at the other woman's expression stilled her tongue. How could she say anything that might dim the proud light in Mattie's eyes?

"Jack and I are just friends," she said instead. "We're really too different to be anything more." She hoped the words would discourage Mattie's matchmaking ideas once and for all.

"I'm sure Jack knows other women who interest him romantically far more than I ever would. In fact, he mentioned plans for that very evening the last time he was over. I'm sure he meant a date."

To her surprise, the news didn't seem to reassure Mattie—quite the opposite. Crinkly worry lines pinched the older woman's forehead.

"Is that right?" she fumed, surprising Cassie further. "I hope it's not the flighty blonde who's been after him. Jack never did show a lick of sense where beautiful women are concerned."

Cassie was trying without success to beat down the flames of jealousy that threatened to engulf her. What flighty blonde?

Then, as if embarrassed by her own outburst, Mattie patted Cassie's hand. "Don't mind me, dear. I just thought you and Jack would really hit it off. Blame it on a mother's wishful thinking."

Cassie wanted desperately to ask about the blonde, but pride made the words stick in her throat.

Behind her wire-framed glasses, Mattie's eyes were twinkling with an expression that didn't seem to go with the resignation in her voice, but Cassie dismissed the little niggle of suspicion that tugged at her attention. Surely Mattie realized she had a better chance to marry Jack off if she promoted someone he had more in common with, someone with no social conscience.

Cassie wondered why the idea made her feel nauseated.

Two days later Cassie was just running her column off on the printer connected with her computer when the phone rang. Hoping it wasn't Bonnie calling her to another protest, she picked up the receiver.

"Cassie, dear," implored the weak voice at the other end. "Could you come over? I feel faint and a little dizzy, and I'm all alone here. I hate to ask . . ." Mattie's words trailed off, followed by a shaky sigh.

"Do you want me to call a doctor? An aid car?" Cassie's fingers gripped the receiver tightly as she tried to remember something, anything about high blood pressure from the first aid course she'd taken several years before.

"No, dear, if you'd just come over until my husband gets back." If anything, Mattie's voice sounded even more frail.

"Of course, I'll be right there." Cassie slammed down the phone and raced next door. After a light knock, she entered Mattie's living room.

"In here, dear." The voice came from the kitchen where Mattie was hunched at the table, next to the telephone.

"Let me help you to the couch. Are you feeling any better? Do you want some water?" Cassie helped the older woman to the living room, noticing how thin she was.

"Some ice water would be nice. There're lemon wedges in the fridge if you wouldn't mind." Already Mattie's voice seemed stronger. Lemon wedges?

Cassie was relieved. "Do you want me to call anyone? Fred, perhaps?" She thought of Mattie's husband.

"No, dear," Mattie said, accepting the glass of water. "He'll be along, if you don't mind waiting. I just hate being by myself at times like this."

"Of course, I understand perfectly, and it's no bother at all. Does this happen often?"

"No, dear, not often. You're a sweet child." Mattie's voice sounded almost normal.

A few moments had passed, and Cassie was plumping a pillow behind the other woman's head when she heard a familiar sound in the driveway. She glanced at Mattie's face just in time to see a smile that was quickly hidden.

"That's Jack's truck!" Cassie peered out the window to be sure. The green half ton screeched to a stop, and Jack leaped from the cab.

"Did I forget to mention that I called him?"

Cassie was torn between relief that Mattie apparently wasn't in real danger and amusement at the naughty expression on her face. Cassie was too used to her mother's plots to be really annoyed.

"I guess you did forget," she replied in what she hoped was a normal voice. "Now that he's here, you don't need me."

Mattie jerked forward, then seemed to catch herself. She fell against the cushions, hand over her heart. "Don't go," she gasped. "A woman needs another woman with her at times like this."

Cassie didn't know if she should laugh or applaud.

Jack, who had just burst through the door, barely glanced at Cassie before rushing to his mother's side.

"What the hell's happening?" he demanded, going down on one knee and grabbing her hand.

Cassie watched with interest to see how Mattie planned to get out of this one.

Chapter Seven

Are you all right?" Jack's voice was full of concern as he rubbed the back of Mattie's hand. "What happened?"

She patted his arm reassuringly with her free hand as Cassie watched with interest, almost sure now that Mattie had been fine all along.

"I just felt a little dizzy, dear," Mattie was saying. "But Cassie rushed right over, and now I'm much better. And I'm so glad you were at your office and not out somewhere riding around."

"There's a phone in my truck, Mom, you know that."

"Yes, I know, but I can never get used to the idea." Mattie attempted to rise.

"You should rest a little longer," Jack said. "I'll call Doc Camber."

Cassie wondered if Jack noticed the look of pure alarm that crossed Mattie's face at his words.

"No, no, Jack. I'll just take a little nap in the bedroom until Dad gets home. You and Cassie could keep each other company if you don't mind staying." She got up slowly, then turned at the doorway. "You do have the time, don't you?"

Jack's expression was turning stern and dangerous as he obviously began to smell a setup. Cassie felt like laughing over the whole incident, but it was clear from the way Jack's thick brows were drawn together into a thunderous frown that humor wasn't the emotion he was experiencing.

"Let me help you," she said to Mattie quickly. So far the big lout hadn't even spoken to Cassie, and she didn't know what she was going to say if he did. He obviously wasn't as happy to see her as she had been to hear his truck and to see him walk in, so broad shouldered and utterly masculine.

At the bedroom door, Mattie paused, her gaze searching Cassie's anxiously. "I'll be fine," she said. "Why don't you get Jack a beer from the fridge. I'm afraid he looks as if he could use some cooling off."

The twinkle in her eyes had been replaced by worry, and Cassie wanted to reassure her, even if her meddling wasn't doing any good.

"You rest. I'll take care of Jack."

The words didn't come out as she'd meant them to, but they certainly reassured Mattie, whose expression perked up immediately. "Thank you, dear," she said. "I'll just close this door, and I'll be asleep in minutes. Once I am, nothing short of an air raid would disturb me."

Cassie was tempted to say something, but the door shut gently before she could figure out a way to warn Mattie that she mustn't continue to interfere in their lives. Oh, well, Jack's mother would have to realize soon enough that he and Cassie would *never* be more than sometimes friendly opponents.

What a depressing thought.

While Jack was waiting for Cassie to return from the bedroom, he helped himself to a can of beer and downed it in three long gulps. He'd been going over a job bid when he'd gotten his mother's call and had dropped everything to race over here.

A popping noise distracted him from his thoughts, and he looked down to see that his fingers had crumpled the empty beer can. Muttering a curse, he tossed it into the garbage and reached for another, then hesitated. He still had to go back to the office and double-check those figures.

Cassie stuck her head into the kitchen. "She's resting, and she said she can sleep through anything." Cassie's delicate features were alive with humor, making Jack wonder what hand she might have had in this obvious wild-goose chase he'd been drawn into.

"Did you put her up to calling me?" he demanded before he'd really thought the question through.

As he stared hard at her, Cassie's face got alarmingly red, and she eyed his shin as if she would like to give him another bruise. Instinctively Jack backed up.

Cassie saw him through a red haze. "You conceited cretin! No one but the great Jack Hoffman would come up with such an idea!" She was so angry she could barely get the words out. "I didn't know she'd called you, too, until I heard your truck."

Cassie advanced upon Jack until they were almost nose to nose. Her head was thrown back, and her breasts rose and fell with each agitated breath. Steam seemed to be coming out her ears and smoke from her nostrils.

"I was going to offer to stay with her until your father gets home," she continued, "but I think I'll leave you to it. *I* have to go home and get back to my *scheming* and *planning*." She emphasized each word with an angry jab of her finger at his chest.

She paused, raking in a deep breath, but before Jack could think of anything suitable to say, she'd whirled away. He followed her to the front door, but she hurried through it without looking back, slamming the screen door behind her.

Damn, she was cute when she was mad.

He called her name twice, but she ignored him as she hurried across the driveway.

Cassie stomped back to her own house, tears of anger and frustration flooding her eyes. Jack had made it crystal clear when he first got to Mattie's that he wasn't the least bit happy to see Cassie, and then he'd actually accused her of setting the whole thing up. Oooh, she couldn't remember ever having been so furious.

Without slowing up she went through to the backyard and grabbed a shovel. She'd turned under a whole row of yellowing pea vines before she began to calm down.

Although Cassie was beginning to wonder if they had a snowball's chance of succeeding, she was glad to assemble with the rest of the picketers the next day. Nothing would make her happier than the chance to conk Jack Hoffman right on his hard hat with her sign.

She'd called Mattie before she left the house, just to make sure the older woman was feeling okay. Neither of them had mentioned Jack or the fact that Cassie had left so quickly and noisily. Maybe the total failure of Mattie's plan would dissuade her from attempting anything further.

Cassie was getting bored with walking back and forth along the front of the job site when several cars pulled up, spilling more picketers. They were carrying crudely lettered signs that said Bring Us Jobs and We Welcome Yano Corp. It was obvious that these new people supported Jack's project.

The two opposing groups squared off, eyeing each other with bristling hostility. Cassie could feel the temperature drop as she stared into the faces across from her. The picketers, mostly men, were all casually, even shabbily dressed, and their expressions were grim.

Finally the tense silence was broken by one of the few women in the other group. "You go home," she shouted, "and quit trying to make trouble. We *want* this company here."

A shout of agreement went up from the others surrounding her, then someone from Cassie's group yelled back. "We were here first, and we're not leaving."

Cassie was getting a little nervous at the violence that simmered all around her. Recognizing a man who lived down at the end of her road and a woman who was trying to support her family by working at the library part-time, Cassie began to wonder if saving a patch of marshland was really worth the pain of dividing a community.

There was more shouting, and several cars stopped, including a truck full of rough-looking men who quickly joined the milling crowd. Someone bumped Cassie, and she dropped her sign. Before she could pick it up, a heavy work boot stepped squarely on it and twisted, wrinkling the cardboard.

"Hey!" she exclaimed, then faltered at the fierceness she saw in the small, bloodshot eyes that glared back at her.

"Go home," the man snarled. He raised his voice and waved a length of two-by-four he'd been carrying at Cassie's group. "All of you, go home!"

When Jack drove down the street and saw the number of people at the entrance to the lot, he was surprised. Then he spotted Cassie's bright little car parked along the curb and his gut twisted. This was no peaceful demonstration, it was a mob, and knowing Cassie, she'd be right in the middle of it.

Relentlessly he drove through the ever-growing mass of people, searching for her dark head. When he saw her, practically butting heads with a big ape who looked like the leader of a biker gang, Jack slammed on his brakes and leaped from the truck.

"That's Hoffman!" someone shouted. "He owns the construction company."

Jack shook off the hands that grabbed at him as he pushed through the crowd. "Cassie!" His only thought was to get her out of there.

When Cassie saw him advancing, face contorted with anger, she gripped the handle of her damaged sign tighter and swallowed the lump that threatened to block her throat. What did he want with her? He called her name again, and she realized that now everyone would know she was acquainted with the enemy.

Turning her back, she tried to slip past two of the older members of her group who were singing some patriotic song from World War I in wavery voices. Misunderstanding her intentions, one of them threw an arm around her shoulder, effectively halting her progress.

"Let her go." Jack's voice behind them was a growl of pure menace.

Old Mr. McMurtry's bifocal-distorted eyes widened, and he tried to untangle his arm from Cassie's.

Before she could move away, Jack reached out to grab her, his fingers biting into her waist. Cassie dropped her sign and let out a yelp of fear as she felt herself being lifted through the air, but her exclamation was rudely cut off by the force with which Jack flung her over his shoulder.

"Put me down!" She couldn't believe this was happening. People from both sides had stopped their arguing and shouting, and were all staring at her as she hung inelegantly across Jack's broad back like a sack of locally grown potatoes. She beat at him with her fists and attempted to kick him, but one muscular arm pinned her legs. His other hand rested squarely on her bottom, burning through the fabric of her shorts.

By the time Jack had threaded his way back to the truck, Cassie had managed to exhaust her entire repertoire of cusswords, which wasn't all that extensive, and had started on threats to his person and his reputation. Her voice was getting hoarse from shouting, but he hadn't uttered a single word.

He intended to get her into his truck and take her out of there before real violence erupted, then to call the police on his car phone. When he looked up and saw the side of his truck, he faltered to a stop.

By the time Jack realized he'd loosened his hold on Cassie, she'd managed to push against him hard enough to slide down his body to the ground. He was still too stunned by the sight before him to appreciate the sensation.

Cassie straightened unsteadily, still furious at his manhandling. "You macho bully," she ranted, having used up all her more-colorful descriptions. "I'd like to..." Her voice trailed off when she saw that he wasn't paying any attention to her, and then her gaze followed the direction of his.

"Oh my God!" She looked from the brutally bashed-in fender to the faces of the people surrounding them. "Who did this?"

One by one they turned away, refusing to meet her eyes. She knew that someone must have seen what happened, but it was obvious from their expression that nobody dared to speak up.

"I'm sorry," she said to Jack, touching his arm. She was so shocked that anyone would carry things this far and deliberately ram his truck that her fury drained away unnoticed.

Jack was glaring down at her, his face pale beneath his tan. "That could have been *you* that someone hurt," he said in a strained voice. "*Now* will you let me take you out of here before these idiots decide to really rumble?"

"Surely there was a witness—" she began, glancing around once again.

"Let the police and my insurance company sort it out. For now, get in the truck."

He was still being high-handed, his tone totally arrogant, but Cassie was surprised to find his protective streak rather endearing and the bulky strength of his body reassuring. Of course, when she came to her senses she'd be madder than a race car driver with a flat tire, but for now she climbed behind the wheel and slid over without further argument.

As she fastened her seat belt, Jack pushed in after her and started the engine, ignoring the shouts behind them. As soon as he and Cassie were back on the street, he called the police on his mobile phone to alert them to the potentially dangerous situation that was brewing.

"Just why did you do that to me?" she demanded the second he'd finished his call. "You made both of us look like fools, and you had no right—"

Jack silenced her with a burning glance. "I had every right."

She waited a moment, but he didn't continue. Had he come on like Errol Flynn because he was afraid for her safety? The idea sent a curious flush of heat dancing across her skin as the corners of her lips crept upward in a little smile. Then she remembered the humiliating way he'd hauled her out of there, ignoring her repeated requests that he put her down. That wasn't caring, it was control, and she wanted no part of it.

"I'd like to know who gave you that right," she began again, thrusting out her chin.

His chill gaze flicked over her with the sting of a cat-o'-nine-tails. "For an intelligent woman you can be incredibly stupid," he said before pressing down the accelerator with his foot.

Did he mean what she wanted to think he meant, or was he referring to the fact that the project was his responsibility? That wouldn't explain why he'd picked on her to carry off, unless he thought she was the ringleader. Cassie rubbed at her forehead, which was beginning to throb with the blows of a hundred hammers.

"You'd do better to worry about your friends back at Little Bighorn than to dwell on your exit," he continued. "At least you're out of there with your hide intact."

Ashamed, Cassie realized she hadn't given the others a thought since Jack had shoved her into the truck. "Do you think they'll be okay? Perhaps we should go back."

"No way! The police are probably sending everyone home right now."

Cassie pressed her lips together, beginning to tremble in a delayed reaction to the ugly turn the crowd had taken. Suddenly the crusade seemed much more serious and complicated than it had when she first thought about saving the homes of some wild creatures from the bulldozer's blade.

Remembering the damage to Jack's fender, she studied his expression. This was definitely not a good time to remind him that her brother owned a body repair shop. He looked violent enough to straighten the twisted fender with his bare hands.

"I'm taking you home," he said into the silence. "If you have any sense, you'll stay there."

The arrogance of his tone made Cassie's hackles rise, then her eyes widened with horror. "Oh, no!" she moaned. "My car's back there." She could picture her beloved bug squashed like an empty tomato can.

Jack sighed. "I'll get one of my men to bring the car to your house." His tone suggested she was becoming a total pain in the behind.

"Don't put yourself out," she snapped.

"I already have."

"And I suppose you're waiting for me to thank you?"

He slowed and turned a corner. "*I'm* not the obtuse one here," he said. "The last thing I expect is thanks."

Cassie crossed her arms over her chest and lapsed into offended silence. What did he mean by that? She felt badly about the damage to his truck, but that didn't mean he could insult her.

"Don't worry," he said, misinterpreting her silence. "I'm sure that *your* car is in no danger."

"You don't think it was one of *my people* who rammed your truck?" She was shocked.

"*Your people* are the ones who want me out of there."

She hated to admit it, but he had a point.

With a last, burning glance as she hopped from the cab, he held out his hand for her car keys and reversed from the driveway.

Later, when Cassie emerged from a cooling shower and peeked out the window, the events of the afternoon replaying over and over in her head like a B movie, she was greatly relieved to see her car sitting in front of the house. She threw on some clothes and went outside to check it for damages.

Cassie was circling her Volkswagen, stroking its shiny fenders and talking in soothing tones, when Jack's truck came back down the street and pulled into her driveway. She put aside the questions that still buzzed in her head at his parting comments and went forward to thank him for delivering the Bug safely.

Jack had been on his way back to the office when he'd remembered an earlier remark of Cassie's that she had a brother who did body and fender work. That was as good an excuse as any to return to her house and find out whether she had decided to be sensible and stay away from the construction site. He had tried telling himself that that was the only reason he wanted to see her.

"Hoffman, you're an idiot," he said to his reflection in the rearview mirror.

Now he stared through the windshield at Cassie's trim figure in brief shorts and a snug tank top that clearly outlined her curves as his fingers gripped the door handle. The thought of what could have happened to her in that mob made his stomach do a slow roll as he stepped from the truck.

"Thanks for bringing my car," she said, lacing her fingers together. Jack couldn't help but remember that not long ago he might have taken her in his arms and greeted her with a kiss. So much had changed between them before they'd even had a chance to really get to know each other. Instead of pulling her into an embrace, he made do with a searching exploration of her wide, dark eyes.

"You okay?" His voice was gruff. "No aftereffects from the riot?"

"It wasn't really a riot. I'm sure nothing like that will happen again."

Impatience surged through him. "What are you, a naive little flower child dabbling in bleeding heart causes? A lot of those people are desperate, and they won't stop at some minor property damage."

Cassie pushed the hair back from her forehead with a hand that trembled. "There's no point in rehashing this. Why did you come back?"

Jack shuffled his feet and ducked his head, almost as if he were embarrassed about something. "Didn't you say that your brother owns a body shop? It would save me some time if I didn't have to take the truck into Sacramento to have it fixed." He indicated the cruel gash in the smooth metal, wincing at the damage.

Cassie hesitated, knowing how busy her brother was. It wasn't likely that he'd make the time to repair Jack's fender unless she asked him to herself.

"Come on in," she said on a resigned sigh. "I'll call and see if he's still there."

Cassie shifted her weight from one foot to the other and glanced at her watch for about the fifth time. They'd been at the shop for almost an hour, after Tom and Jack had hit it off like long lost army buddies.

While Cassie had been trying not to gawk at the long, powerful muscles in Jack's thighs as he leaned against a workbench, Tom had showed them a restored Mustang he was pinstriping for the owner of a local gym. Jack's admiration of its etched windows had prompted a discussion of possible designs for the rear window of his truck.

Then, after they'd handled the arrangements to fix the fender, Tom made a casual comment about the local track meet the next evening. Before Cassie knew what was happening, the two men were swapping stories about their own high school teams. Without missing a beat, they'd gone on to football while Cassie stood listening to the deep, husky timbre of Jack's voice.

"Did you play any college ball?" Tom asked.

"No, I wrecked my knee in high school."

Cassie's gaze followed the line of his leg to the bend in his jeans. She didn't remember his knees looking anything less than perfect.

Tom shook his head sympathetically. "Damn shame." He looked down at his watch. "I've got to get going."

"Heavy date?" Cassie couldn't resist asking.

"I don't think Mom would appreciate being called 'heavy,'" Tom replied. "I'm due over there for dinner, and I've got to clean up first."

"Sorry we kept you so long," Jack said, stretching out one big hand. "I appreciate your making time for the truck, and I'll have it here day after tomorrow."

Tom shook Jack's outstretched hand, then turned to Cassie. "Denny had to cancel our plans to go waterskiing—something wrong with the motor on the boat. Let's get together soon anyway, okay?"

Cassie returned his smile. "Come for dinner one night this week."

Tom flicked a glance at Jack before answering. "Maybe we could make it a foursome."

An awkward silence fell, then Tom, obviously realizing he'd put his foot in his mouth, pressed onward in a teasing tone. "I'll come if you promise not to fix anything with tofu in it. And you know how I feel about those greens you swear by."

Cassie playfully punched his arm. "I could barbecue some chicken," she said. "That should satisfy your lust for animal flesh."

Promising to call him later, Cassie turned to leave with Jack. It was obvious the two men had hit it off, and that would only complicate things. Tom could be as bad as their mother with his clumsy machinations.

"Who's Denny?" Jack asked as soon as they were out of earshot.

"A friend of Tom's I've never even met." Cassie was pleased that he was curious enough to ask.

"Ah." Jack didn't speak again until they were on the road. "How about something to eat, then I'll take you by my construction company," he suggested after a long but not uncomfortable silence. "It's too late to go back to work, and I missed lunch."

Cassie had been watching the movements of his hands on the steering wheel and the way the light was caught in the fine dusting of gold hairs on his forearms. She wasn't about to admit that she wasn't hungry, pleased that he wanted to prolong their time together. Hesitating, she studied his expression, wondering if it was possible to keep their professional differences separate from the very personal draw she felt toward him whenever they got within touching distance.

The expression in Jack's blue eyes was screened by his thick lashes as he waited for her answer. One hand hovered above her knee, then returned to the steering wheel.

Pleasure burst within Cassie at his offer to show her where he worked. She'd tried to picture him there before and failed. She swallowed and bobbed her head, breaking contact with his intent stare.

"Sure. I'd like to see your business."

The thought popped into Jack's mind that she might be following the motto Know Your Enemy, but then he forced his tightly coiled body to relax. The attraction between them had nothing to do with the protest or anything else environmental. It was physical and emotional, and intensely personal.

"Good," he murmured, putting the truck into gear. "How does pizza sound to you?"

They'd stuffed themselves on a deep-dish, thick-crusted feast laden with cheeses, an assortment of toppings and the best sauce Cassie had ever tasted, washed down with glasses of a red Italian wine. As Jack held open the door of the restaurant, she moaned and rubbed her flat stomach.

"I ate too much."

He slipped an arm around her shoulders as they waited to cross the street. His warmth seeped into Cassie, who had to stifle the impulse to snuggle against his wide chest. "Mario puts the franchises to shame, doesn't he?" Jack asked.

It took Cassie a moment to gather her scattered senses and decipher who Mario might be. Of course, the restaurant they'd just left.

"Mmm," she agreed. "He's a genius. That was better than the pizza I make myself."

When he'd joined her in the truck, he turned, key in hand. "Modest, aren't you?"

She gave him a mock-arrogant stare. "You haven't tasted my pizza sauce yet."

"When can I?"

Cassie wasn't ready to commit herself to seeing Jack again. She should be home right now making sure Bonnie and the others were all okay, not indulging her own romantic notions by spending time with him.

"I'll have to check my schedule and get back to you," she muttered when he continued to wait for an answer.

He didn't comment, but she noticed that the lines bracketing his mouth deepened as its corners turned downward. When he started the truck, the engine raced in protest before he released the pressure of his foot on the accelerator.

They drove toward Sacramento without speaking as Cassie mulled over everything that had been said, wishing she could think of something besides a dinner invitation that would recapture the easy mood they'd shared earlier. As she debated the wisdom of inviting him, Jack slowed and turned into a gravel driveway, stopping before a gate next to a small, attractive office building.

A short, wizened man in a green uniform came forward. "Hi, boss," he said as he opened the gate in the cyclone fencing. "Workin' late?" Then he spotted Cassie, and one wrinkled hand touched his cap. "Evenin', ma'am."

As Cassie smiled a greeting, Jack introduced them. "Herb Applebaum, Cassie Culpepper. Herb's been with me for years."

The guard shut the gate behind them, then walked over to the truck, opening the passenger door before Jack could get to it and reaching up a hand to assist Cassie to the ground.

"Thank you." She noticed that his eyes were twinkling.

"Interested in construction, are you?"

She glanced quickly at Jack, then back to Herb's deeply lined face.

"Umm, yes. I find it fascinating."

"Come on," Jack said, knowing that the old man was capable of keeping them there for an hour and not willing to share Cassie for a tenth of that time. "I'll show you around inside first."

As Cassie allowed him to capture her hand in his, Jack turned back to Herb. "We'll see you before we leave."

Herb took the hint and touched his fingers to his cap again. "Sure thing."

Cassie seemed impressed as she followed him around, listening carefully to his explanations. Inside the building there were two private offices, a reception area and a large room containing four desks with computer terminals as well as a bank of file cabinets. Maps and architect's renderings covered every available wall.

Jack was proud of the company he'd started and watched over as carefully as he would a child, but he wondered if Cassie would see that or if she would dismiss his efforts with as little understanding as he had her ladybugs. Even now, the memory of his callousness made him wince.

"I recognize the condominiums where you live," she exclaimed, pointing to a full-color framed drawing.

"This is the new plant for Yano." Jack gestured to a detailed sketch of the complex, but Cassie glanced without comment.

After a small hesitation, he sighed and looked at the large wall clock.

"I'll show you around outside before it gets dark. Would you like some coffee first?"

Cassie nodded, then watched as he quickly filled the drip pot and turned it on. She was admiring the graceful way he moved and the wide sweep of his shoulders when the phone rang, making her jump.

"I'd better answer that," Jack said. "Excuse me."

After a moment he covered the receiver with his hand. "I'm sorry but it's my foreman. I'll be a few minutes. Would you pour the coffee and take Herb some with two sugars while you're waiting? I'll be out as soon as I can."

Cassie was almost grateful to get away. Something about the deserted office in the evening quiet had made her achingly aware of him, and she needed some air. "Take your time." She was sure that Herb would be willing to show her around outside. When they'd first pulled in, she had noticed several huge pieces of equipment that aroused her curiosity.

Herb's tour of the yard included a character endorsement of Jack that sounded as if the younger man had written it himself. The watchman seemed to be under the impression that Cassie and his boss were a couple. Ignoring her attempts to convince him otherwise, Herb went on to tell her what a fine, honest and caring employer Jack had been as they stopped to look at a grader whose back tire stood higher than Cassie's head.

"Gave me a job, you know," Herb said. "Eight years ago when I crawled out of an empty muscatel bottle and no one else would trust me. If it wasn't for Jack I'd be back on the street now, or worse."

Cassie didn't know what to say. She had wondered if Jack really needed a security guard since some kind of alarm system would surely do an adequate job. Now she understood. It presented a side of him she hadn't seen before. Or perhaps she just hadn't looked hard enough.

"He's helped others, too, when they've gotten hurt or he's had to lay them off," Herb continued after taking a slurp of his coffee. "Carried one young fellow through the slack time cuz his wife was expecting. Johnny was pulling laborer's wages to do handyman chores around here till things picked up again."

Before Cassie could think of a comment, she heard Jack's voice calling her name. Herb walked back toward the office with her.

"Sorry about the phone call," Jack apologized again. "Did Herb tell you everything about bulldozers you ever wanted to know?"

Cassie gazed at him with new warmth, knowing instinctively that he'd be greatly embarrassed to know what Herb had told her. "Actually we had a very nice visit, and I'm impressed with your business."

Jack stared down at her, a pleased expression on his face. "I'm glad."

Cassie remembered the time she'd shown Jack around her business and how defensively she'd behaved toward his suggestions. Now she could see that he did have a considerable amount of expertise to share, and she felt slightly sheepish for her prickly attitude. Jack's face gave no hint whether he, too, was remembering that conversation as they said goodbye to Herb and drove back toward Cassie's house.

When Jack took her hand and placed it high on his thigh, she forgot all about bulldozers and bugs, wondering instead if he was going to kiss her when they got back to her place. Cassie was torn between wishing the drive was shorter so she could find out, and wanting it never to end, so she could continue to feel the smooth workings of his big muscles against the flat of her hand and the body heat that radiated toward her in the soft twilight.

Chapter Eight

When they pulled into her driveway, Cassie found herself automatically glancing next door to see if the Hoffmans' cars were there. Then she silently chided herself, ignoring the relief she felt seeing that one was gone and that there weren't any lights on in the house. She was an adult, and she absolutely refused to sneak around!

"Want to come in for a minute?" She didn't quite meet Jack's gaze as she issued what she hoped sounded like a casual invitation. His company during the past several hours had made her more aware than ever of the pull between them, and she wasn't ready to see him go.

"Yes." Jack's reply was decisive. When his warm arm curled possessively around her waist and he hauled her up next to him so that their hips bumped gently as they walked, Cassie wondered if she'd made a big mistake.

As Jack entered Cassie's living room, he spotted one of the cats asleep on the couch. He moved closer and noticed the red collar identifying the female of the pair as Crystal opened one brilliant blue eye, then the other.

Cassie said something about calling Bonnie as Jack leaned over and chucked Crystal under the chin before sitting down next to the lazy cat. Crystal immediately rose and stretched, then curled up in his lap.

Cassie returned a few minutes later. "The police sent everybody home," she said. "Apparently no one got hurt."

"What did you tell Bonnie about me?" His fingers were scratching Crystal's throat.

"You?"

"About leaving with me. Didn't she ask?"

Cassie began toying with a strand of her hair. "Well, she did ask if I was okay, and I told her I was."

"Is that all?" It was difficult not to grin at her confusion.

"No, but I didn't feel like trying to explain everything." She was beginning to sound defensive.

"That's an explanation I'd like to hear," Jack said dryly before returning his attention to the cat.

Cassie walked over to the couch. "Crystal likes you."

He wasn't sure if Cassie approved, but he smiled anyway. "Of course. She has good taste."

Cassie sat down next to him, her fingers idly stroking Crystal's ears. "Cats have very small brains."

"But good instincts." As he shifted toward Cassie, Crystal gave a disgusted cry and leaped to the floor, jerking her tail disdainfully as she stalked off.

Gazing into Jack's eyes, which were narrowed with suppressed laughter, Cassie cast about for something else to say, but her own brain seemed to have shrunk to the size of a domestic feline's. All she could think about was how rivetingly attractive Jack was and how very much she wanted him to kiss her.

She swayed closer. Something in his eyes changed abruptly, and he leaned back against the couch, sucking in a deep breath. "Here, kitty, kitty, kitty," he called to Blake, who was standing in the doorway.

Cassie turned toward the cat with less enthusiasm than usual. Jack had begun to scratch his fingers on the edge of the couch, and Blake was creeping forward, eyes dilated.

"Look at Crystal," Jack instructed, barely moving his lips.

Cassie glanced at the other cat, who was stalking Blake's switching tail.

"Can't take your eyes off a woman for a minute," Jack muttered, still wiggling his fingers, "or they blindside you."

Blake coiled to spring at his target. Cassie sat very still, watching Crystal. As Blake moved, the other cat launched herself at him. Blake jumped and the two silver bodies rolled across the carpet in a tangle, biting and growling. Then, as if the move had been choreographed, they sprang apart, backs arched.

A low growl rolled from Crystal's throat as she froze in an awkwardly twisted pose. Only her tail flicked as Blake crouched. Their eyes were locked. As if on cue, they leaped again.

"Won't they hurt each other?" Jack asked.

"I guess not. They play like this all the time, and I can never tell if they're having an argument or just kidding around."

Blake finally lost patience and sprang at Crystal. She reared up, thumping his head several times with lightning jabs of her front paw. Blake, who'd apparently had enough, ran out of the room, tail fluffed out like a bottle brush. Crystal sat back on her haunches and began to wash the paw that had touched his head.

Jack burst out laughing. "That says it all, doesn't it? What an expression of absolute superiority."

"Of course. She *is* the female of the pair." Cassie couldn't resist a little teasing. "She usually wins."

The lone dimple in Jack's cheek appeared as he returned her smile. "Think you're superior, do you?" His tone should have warned Cassie, who continued to grin.

"Absolutely."

With a sudden movement his arms clamped around her, and before Cassie could draw a startled breath she was pulled across his muscular thighs, her head tilted back to stare into his smug face.

"What's your next move, boss?" he teased.

"Well, I wasn't talking about brute strength," she managed to say, voice only slightly shaky.

"Neither was I." There was laughter in his eyes as his head lowered.

Cassie's lids drifted shut as his mouth touched hers, then lifted away. She sighed as he returned, lips warm, mustache as soft as a drift of silk. Cassie was vaguely aware of the powerful arms holding her close as she absorbed the pressure of his mouth, savoring the kiss. Her fingers curled into the front of his shirt as Jack took them deeper, his tongue teasing her lips apart before sliding roughly against hers.

Beneath her palm Cassie could feel the drumming of his heart, even and heavy. He smelled of warm, clean male and a faint, masculine cologne she had come to associate with him. She curled one arm around his neck and nestled even closer as his mouth continued to work blissful magic on her own.

Just as the world began to spin crookedly, Jack groaned and lifted his head. "I've missed you," he breathed unsteadily, nuzzling her ear.

Cassie's voice was thin and light as she replied. "Me, too." She'd missed the closeness and everything about him. Somewhere along the line, despite her most logical arguments with herself, she'd fallen in love with Jack Hoffman.

She managed a tremulous smile as the truth of her feelings hit her, and he bent his head again, stringing kisses down her cheek and across her jaw. His warm breath was an additional caress as she placed a hand against his face, urging him back to her mouth. When he complied, she touched the very tip of her tongue to his upper lip, tickling the edge of his mustache and making him shudder as he captured her mouth in a hard kiss.

"Witch," he said against her lips. His voice had thickened and his breathing was shallow. Cassie's own control splintered as she pressed against him. The driving need to be ever closer, the need she'd tried to ignore for so long was expanding like a living being, threatening to take her over.

The small part of her mind still capable of rational thought wondered if that would be so bad. It had been easy in the past to keep men at a distance, but when she was with Jack she came alive in a totally new way. Her body throbbed in secret places and she felt light-headed and strangely empty. It was gloriously obvious that Jack, too, was adrift in the same sea of passion when he groaned deep in his throat and pulled her even closer.

The kiss went on and on, making Cassie realize how many different emotions a kiss could show. Her arms tightened around Jack as he shifted from gentle persuasion to overwhelming insistence. Again and again he molded his lips to hers, stroking and caressing her sensitive flesh with his tongue until she felt she'd either melt or die.

Her fingers played idly with the hair at the back of his neck as she savored the new emotions he was arousing within her. He lifted his mouth, opening his clouded eyes to gaze down at her, as a hard tremor shook him. Then he turned his head, rubbing his cheek against her caressing hand. She tugged at a lock of his hair, then tunneled her fingers through it, enjoying the warmth of his scalp.

"Mmm," Jack purred in a throaty voice as she continued to move her fingers through the hair on his nape. "That feels so— *Youch!*"

He straightened abruptly, his hands releasing Cassie and grabbing at the back of his neck. Her grip tightened as she tried to keep from rolling onto the floor, her arms locked around his neck. Cassie felt warm fur against her fingers.

Before she could brace herself further, Jack shot up from the couch, breaking her embrace and spilling her to the carpet in a graceless heap.

"Damn," he howled. "Get this creature off me!"

As Cassie scrambled to her feet, rubbing an elbow she'd banged on the table leg, she realized what had happened. Thinking that her shifting fingers on Jack's nape signaled another game, Blake had pounced on his wide back. When Jack moved abruptly, Blake hung on for dear life, all twenty claws digging in.

Jack was hunched over, instinctively trying to provide Blake with a wide enough perch so that he'd release his painful grip. "Damn, damn, damn," Jack muttered through clenched teeth.

Before Cassie could reach for the frightened animal, Blake made his own bid for freedom, leaping to the back of the couch and beyond, probably ending up deep in Cassie's closet, in the empty shoe box where he liked to hide when things got scary.

"Let me see," Cassie said, gently turning Jack around as he slowly straightened. There were several snags in the back of his tan shirt. "I'd better check the scratches."

Jack moved gingerly. Blake's landing had taken his mind off Cassie and the passion she stirred in him with an abruptness that had sucked the breath from his throat. One moment he'd been completely involved in her warmth and the sweet honey of her lips, the next it was as if live coals had been dumped on him. His back felt as if the devil himself had run across it, branding him with burning hoofprints.

"Come into the kitchen and take off your shirt."

When he stared at Cassie, she turned bright red, then whirled away. "I need to see the damage," she snapped over her shoulder.

Mulling over her reaction, Jack followed her into the other room, releasing buttons as he went.

When he'd peeled off the garment, Cassie indicated a chair, touched his warm skin with one hand and jerked it away as if *she'd* been burned.

"Am I scarred for life?" he asked, his sense of humor beginning to return as she clucked her tongue.

"It's not as bad as I thought it would be." Cassie hoped that Jack would attribute the breathiness of her voice to shock over what had happened. She hadn't really forgotten the devastating male beauty of his wide shoulders and tanned skin, but seeing that muscular expanse of flesh once again was enough to make an angel consider bending her halo.

"I'll get the first aid kit," Cassie croaked, turning away before her seeking hands could reach for him again.

Now was not the time to give in to her feminine desires to stroke the dark skin and explore the texture of the crisp hair she'd glimpsed curling against his chest like the finest gold wires.

By the time Cassie returned with a dampened cloth and a tube of medicated cream, the scratches had begun to hurt a little less. Jack's mind had turned back to what they were doing when he'd been attacked, and he stared hard at Cassie's slightly swollen mouth. She walked around behind him in a wide circle.

"Seems like you're always patching me up," he said, tilting his head back so he could see her as she dabbed at him with the cloth.

"This time it wasn't your fault."

"I've given up trying to keep Mom in the dark. It takes too much effort." He didn't add that it did no good, but they both realized as much.

With soothing strokes she spread the cream on his skin, her touch as gentle as the flutter of feathered wings.

"Ever think of being a nurse?" he asked, only half kidding.

"Not really."

"You'd be good at it." He turned around, capturing her restless hands in his and lifting them to his lips. "Angel hands," he murmured, kissing the knuckles.

Cassie was melting inside when she felt the intimate rasp of his tongue against her palm. The sensual caress curled her toes and made her jerk away.

Before she could retreat completely, Jack stood up, towering over her. Shirtless he seemed much more primitive and totally dangerous, as if a civilized shell had split and fallen away. His gaze had narrowed and his face seemed tighter, almost threatening.

Cassie swallowed, her eyes widening.

"Come here." The sound of his words was soft velvet, lined with steel.

"Me?" Her voice cracked.

Jack's gaze was unwavering.

She gulped and stepped forward, completely powerless to resist the magnetic pull.

He took her trembling hands and wrapped them around his waist as she tilted her head with a small moan to meet his descending mouth. His fingers dug into her shoulders, and he bent her head farther back as she melted against him like ice cream on a hot day. Cassie was drowning in sensation, going under for the third time when the loud noise of the doorbell yanked them apart.

"That better not be one of our mothers," Jack growled as he released her.

It wasn't, it was Bonnie.

When Cassie stepped aside to let the other woman in, she glanced at Jack, who'd followed her to the door. Thank goodness he'd put his shirt back on, but she wished he'd buttoned it. Standing there with his weight on one hip and a thumb hooked into his belt, he looked incredibly sexy and rumpled. Cassie swallowed the lump that had formed in her throat as Bonnie halted, mouth all but hanging open.

"I'm sorry," she stammered, staring at Jack. "I didn't know you were busy." She blushed and gestured with one hand. "I didn't mean *busy*, I just meant..." She darted a beseeching glance at Cassie as her words stumbled to an embarrassed halt. "I guess I don't know what I meant."

Jack grinned, the dimple flashing impudently.

Cassie made quick introductions as Bonnie's eyebrows rose in silent inquiry. Of course she knew who Jack was, and her eyes filled with questions as she carefully avoided looking at his open shirt.

"Cassie, I'd better be going." Jack's tone was reluctant.

"I'm sorry about your back," she said, causing her friend's eyebrows to climb even higher, disappearing beneath her bangs. "I'm sure the scratches will heal quickly."

Beside her, Bonnie made a choking sound before hastily stepping out of Jack's way.

"See you later." He included them both, gaze lingering for a burning moment on Cassie. Silently she mourned Bonnie's rotten timing.

"I'm *really sorry*," the other woman said after Jack had left. "Why didn't you just tell me you were busy?"

"We were through." Realizing how conclusive the words sounded, Cassie shook her head and tried again. "It's not what you're thinking. My cat scratched him, and I was putting some disinfectant on his shoulder."

"One of your gentle little kitties scratched him? What did he do?" It was easy to see that Bonnie's imagination was filling in the blanks.

Cassie sighed, leading the way to the kitchen. "It's a long story."

"Yes, I can imagine. Remember that I saw him carry you away from the protest. Cassie, do you know who he really is?"

"Of course I do."

"How did you get mixed up with a rogue like that?" Bonnie's voice was filled with curiosity. "Not that I don't envy you, but he's..."

"I know who he is. But I didn't know he was doing this project until I saw him down there. His mother lives next door." She pointed to Mattie's house.

"Are there any more like him at home?"

It was immediately clear to Cassie that her friend wasn't about to hold Jack's lack of values against him.

"Did you come by for any special reason?" It was time to change the subject and distract Bonnie from her speculation on Cassie's relationship with Jack.

"I just wanted to make sure that you're okay. You sounded so evasive on the phone." She giggled. "I guess I should have waited until tomorrow."

"No, no. Jack really was just leaving."

Bonnie waited a moment, then when it was clear that Cassie wasn't going to elaborate, she rose. "Well, since you seem to be all right, I'd better go. One of these days you'll have to tell me how you and Mr. Hoffman met in the first place." She paused at the door. "If you don't want him for yourself, let me know, okay?" With a bold wink she was gone.

Cassie was relieved that her friend hadn't pressed for an explanation. How could she have possibly told Bonnie why Jack had dragged her away from the site when she didn't fully understand herself? He said it was for her own safety, but she still thought he just didn't like her being on the opposite side. That idea led the way to a whole line of thinking she wasn't ready to deal with yet.

It was easy enough for Cassie to find out from her brother when Jack was scheduled to pick up his truck. She and Tom went to breakfast that morning, and it was natural enough for her to return to Auto Art with him to look at his latest project.

"Isn't she wonderful? We just rolled her out of the paint booth last night." Tom was gazing with adoration at the pure lines of the old Studebaker parked before them.

"The paint job's a beauty," Cassie said. "How many coats did you put on?"

"Fourteen."

The car was black, a deep, bottomless black that still looked wet. The interior had been completely redone in black leather and the engine rebuilt before the Studebaker was delivered to Tom's for the bodywork.

In the next bay was Jack's truck, looking as good as new. Cassie walked over to it, trailing her fingers across the repaired fender.

"Hoffman should be here anytime," Tom said. "Should I thank *him* for your breakfast invitation?" His voice held a teasing note. "He *is* why you're here, isn't he?"

"I don't know what you're talking about. Do I have to have a reason to take my only brother to breakfast?" Cassie winced at the defensive tone she could hear in her own voice.

Tom studied her warm cheeks. "You know I'm here for you," he said on a quieter note. "Jack seems like a nice guy, but I don't want you to get hurt."

Before Cassie could reply, Tom turned away as if the words had made him uncomfortable, pushing open the door to the office and letting it swing shut behind him. Cassie released a long, slow sigh of relief. It was bad enough that her intentions had been so transparent, but at least Tom wasn't going to press her about them.

When Jack pulled up in front of Tom's shop with his foreman, John Clearwater, he was surprised to see the polka-dotted VW parked there.

"Want me to wait?"

"No, that's okay. I know the truck's ready." Jack leaped from the cab, almost forgetting to thank John for the lift.

Cassie was the first thing he saw when he walked into the large, open area. He stopped, staring. She wore a pink, stretchy top and cutoffs, and he thought he'd never seen anyone so beautiful in his whole life.

"Hi." Her voice was soft.

Jack forced his hands to stay at his sides as he walked over to her, wondering what she was doing there. "Hi."

She smiled up at him, her dark eyes crinkling at the corners. He glanced at her lips and remembered how they felt pressed against his. The muscles in his arms bunched, and his chest expanded on a deeply indrawn breath.

"I . . ." they said together. As they both stood chuckling, Tom came into the room.

"What do you think?"

Jack glanced at him, uncomprehending.

"The truck. Could you tell which side was hit if you didn't know?"

Jack colored and shook his head. "No, it's great."

Cassie knew he hadn't even glanced at it yet. When he angled his gaze back to her she was studying the newly painted Studebaker coupe.

The two men bent to examine the repair work on the pickup when Cassie joined them. She meant to catch Jack when he got away from Tom and invite him to dinner, a dinner she told herself was merely a simple repayment for the barbecue she'd enjoyed at his house. She was deep in thought about the possible wording of the invitation when Tom broke her concentration.

"Cassie?"

The two men were waiting, obviously expecting her to say something.

"Thinking about the next harvest?" Tom teased.

"Banana squash," she said quickly. "I was thinking about my banana squash."

Tom's expression was skeptical.

"I asked if you could join us," Jack said. "I'm taking Tom out for a steak to thank him for doing such a good job and so quickly. Can you make it?"

"Uh, I guess so. If you're sure—"

"Sounds great," Tom cut in. "First breakfast, now dinner."

Cassie caught his implication immediately as Jack looked puzzled. She glared at Tom, whose grin widened. "Shall we meet you?" he asked.

Jack hesitated as if he wanted to say something, then nodded. "Sure, the steak house on Fifth? Sevenish?"

Tom glanced at Cassie, who bobbed her head. What Jack so casually referred to as a "steak house" was one of the most expensive restaurants in Palmerton, and had the very best prime rib she'd ever bitten into. Her mouth began to water. Whether it was Jack or the food that started her juices flowing she wasn't about to question.

"I'm leaving," she said as Tom preceded Jack into the office to settle the bill. "I'll see you later." Only Jack turned and waved, but his smile was warm.

Cassie had hoped the protest wouldn't come up for discussion that evening, but Tom had run into Bonnie at lunch. To Cassie's dismay, he introduced the subject over dessert.

"Is that one of your building projects?" he asked Jack while Cassie stirred her caramel custard into an unidentifiable swirl.

"Cassie and I both have an interest in it," Jack said dryly. "Haven't you read all about it in the *Bee*?"

Tom set down his fork, pushing the blueberry pie aside and resting a forearm on the table. "I've read some. It's the one that group of picketers has been trying to delay. Something about saving the wetlands for the wild ducks.''

As Jack nodded in agreement, Cassie stabbed her spoon into her silver dessert dish. ''It's more than just ducks,'' she said, heat in her voice. ''There are all kinds of wild animals that make their homes in that area.''

Both Jack and Tom stared, expressions unreadable. ''That industrial complex has predicted almost six hundred new jobs during the next couple of years,'' her brother said. ''Since the mill closed, no big industries have located here, and we need the work.''

Cassie was taken aback by his attitude. ''Steelworkers aren't going to fill the jobs at an electronics plant.''

''They might. Their families might.'' Tom's eyes, so like her own, bored into her. ''Look at the total picture, Cassie. I read about this whole thing in the paper last week, and I saw the last protest on the local news. It turned into a riot, and three people were injured.''

Cassie had heard from Bonnie that several of the rowdy strangers who'd piled out of the back of a rusted-out pickup truck had gotten into a fight among themselves. They'd all been drinking.

''Maybe you can talk some sense into her,'' Jack said. ''If she insists on going back down there, she might get hurt.''

Tom shook his head before addressing Cassie. ''I don't think you've really thought this through, or you wouldn't be trying to stop the new plant.''

His unexpectedly adamant support of the opposing side gave Cassie pause. She'd always respected Tom's opinion, and he cared as much about the environment as she did.

Before she could comment, a short, Oriental man in a silk suit stopped by the table. Jack glanced up, then slid back his chair. "Sam! How are you?"

Cassie recognized the man from several pictures she'd seen in the paper. "You're with the Yano Corporation," she gasped, rising. Beside her, Tom stood, too.

Reluctantly, Jack made the introductions, hoping that Sam would move on before Cassie had time to find a soapbox.

"Mr. Okimoto, have you considered the harm your company is doing to the local ecological balance?" she asked.

Sam glanced at Jack, one dark brow quirked. "Yes, we have done extensive studies," he said. "The location we picked is the only one in the area suitable for our needs."

Cassie's voice went up a little. "What about the needs of the wild creatures you're displacing?" she demanded. "Once that land is covered with concrete and asphalt it can never be restored to its natural state."

"You think Mr. Hoffman does not build things of beauty?" Sam was clearly trying to divert Cassie, but Jack had spent enough time with the other man to know when he was getting annoyed even though he appeared outwardly calm.

"That's not the point," Cassie argued. "What's important—"

Sam bowed his head as if apologizing for his interruption. "I beg your pardon, Miss Culpepper. What is important to me at this time is to join the rest of my party before they become impatient to order their dinners." Before Cassie could utter another word, he turned to Tom.

"It was very nice to meet you both. Enjoy your dessert. Jack, I will see you in the morning." His black eyes glittered, and Jack could hear the underlying grimness in his polite voice. He knew that Sam Okimoto would have questions about his choice of dinner companion, not to mention his sense of loyalty.

When Sam took his seat across the room and the three of them were back in their chairs, an awkward silence fell. Glancing first at Cassie, then at Jack, Tom stood again. "I just remembered a phone call I have to make. Be right back."

"What do you think you were doing?" Jack demanded the moment Tom was out of earshot. "Sam Okimoto's an important client."

Cassie leaned toward him across the table. "I couldn't just smile and pretend I approve of what you're both doing."

Jack groaned and slapped an open hand against his forehead. "Why not? We're here having dinner, not taking a stand on world hunger. Did you have to make a scene? Do you have to turn everything into a life-and-death issue?"

"It is life-and-death!"

"Damn, but you're stubborn!" Their voices had gotten progressively louder until several patrons at neighboring tables turned to stare.

"I didn't make a scene, but you're doing a good job of it right now," Cassie replied, glancing around. "Why don't you shout a little louder?"

"I'll do better than that!" Jack rose, scraping back his chair. He glanced at the check the waiter had left and dropped several bills onto the table. "I'll remove my offensive presence, how about that?"

Chapter Nine

Cassie's cheeks had grown hot with the attention they were receiving. Everyone in the place must know that Jack was walking out on her.

As he swung angrily away, Tom returned to the table. "What's the trouble?" He glanced down at the crumpled bills, then at Jack's flushed face.

Cassie got to her feet. "Tom, please take me home," she requested in a voice as calm as a sheet of ice.

Tom studied Jack's thunderous expression for a moment. "I hope you aren't in a hurry," he said to the other man as Cassie went into shock. "I was just about to ask if you could drop my sister off."

She sucked in an angry breath, but before she could protest Tom spoke again. "Something's come up and I need to go in the opposite direction." He ignored Cassie's death grip on his arm.

Jack stared at Tom, his eyes narrowed so that only a glint of blue showed, then the tension seemed to leak from his big body as Cassie stood by, steaming. "Okay," he agreed after a moment of silent communication that infuriated Cassie even more. "Maybe it would be a good idea, after all."

When she and Jack were in his truck, she couldn't resist one remark about macho loyalty being thicker than water. Noticing Jack's grim expression, she then lapsed into chilly silence.

As he turned onto her street, she broke the stalemated silence. "We'll never agree," she said. "We shouldn't even discuss anything controversial."

"Maybe you should concentrate on your own career," Jack replied, stopping in her driveway, "and pay less attention to mine."

"What on earth do you mean?" Was he telling her to mind her own business?

"If you paid attention to where your own life is headed and the opportunities you've missed, you wouldn't have so much free time to meddle in other people's business."

Cassie scooted to the far end of the wide bench seat, not stopping until the door handle was pressed uncomfortably into her back. "Just what are you talking about?"

"I've been reading your column," he said, surprising her. "I don't know that much about gardening, but your writing makes it interesting and easy to understand." He thought for a moment. "Why aren't you trying to get on a newspaper with a bigger circulation, or whatever it is you do to advance your journalism career, instead of wasting your talents in one local weekly?"

Cassie was flattered that he'd bothered to read her column, but angry at his smug assumption that she was strictly small town and totally without ambition. "I *am* syndicated," she informed him with great satisfaction, "in over *thirty* weeklies all over Northern California."

Jack stared, obviously disconcerted by her news. Was that his opinion of her, a beetle-brained airhead who was content to poke around in the dirt when she wasn't packing cute little bugs into fast-food containers? A brain-dead bimbo who had absolutely no business sense and had to be lectured by a would-be tycoon like himself?

Cassie began to puff up with annoyance. "Instead of trying to manage my career, perhaps you should look to your own conscience." She couldn't resist the dig. "*Some* progressive construction companies are including landscaping and greenbelts in their building projects. *Some* builders actually care about grass and trees, and not just parking lots and profits!"

It was Jack's turn to face her with a superior grin. "If you really knew me, Miss Know-it-all, you'd be aware that I carry a landscape architect on my payroll, and that I've always included *plenty* of plantings around a project. I also save as many trees as possible. Have you forgotten the garden around the pool at my condo that you waxed poetic about?" Triumph made his eyes glitter as Cassie stared at him in confusion. They didn't know each other at all.

"Perhaps next time you get the chance, you'll look a little closer at the plans for the Yano complex. A choice bit of land has been set aside for a nice little park with a reflecting pool where the employees can eat outside when the weather's nice, and we're also thinking about putting in a jogging path."

Cassie's heart had already decided that Jack was a man worthy of her love, but her brain wasn't as easily convinced. Even now, a part of her held back, wanting to believe his words but not entirely convinced.

"What about the spraying company?" she asked, groping to make a point. "You'd still have it if it wasn't for that tax benefit you mentioned before."

Jack sighed and ran a hand across his forehead. He'd known that slight bending of the truth would come back to haunt him. It had all been a stupid attempt to save his pride because he hadn't wanted to admit that Cassie was right about the pesticides causing the rash on his arms.

He looked at her tense body huddled against the passenger door, eyes watchful, mouth thinned into an uncompromising line.

"Oh, Cassie, what have I done?" he murmured. When he proceeded to tell her exactly why he'd disbanded Sierra, her eyes grew wider and so did her smile.

"Why didn't you tell me?" she bubbled, sliding closer. "I couldn't figure out why your explanation sounded suspect, but it was so obvious that you didn't want to discuss the subject."

He wondered if she had noticed that she'd moved so close that one rounded breast was pushing softly against his upper arm. For one heady moment he wished he owned some other small businesses he could close down, if it made her that happy.

"I admit it wasn't the brightest thing I've ever done," he confessed, trying not to move the arm that was beginning to burn from its contact with her. "I guess I just didn't want to hear you say 'I told you so.' Anyway, that's old news. There are other things in our way now."

Cassie had just noticed that she was pressed intimately against him. The tip of her breast hardened in response to his warmth, and his words barely registered as she tried to ease away, glad he wasn't the irresponsible pirate she had thought.

She should have realized all along that Jack was kind and responsible and caring. His own security guard had shown her that and so had the way Jack cared for his parents. Not every bachelor son would put up with his mother's meddling or take time away from a busy schedule to mow their lawn. Instead of remembering things like that, Cassie had gotten caught up in this project and had allowed herself to think the worst.

"Look," he said as she remained silent, "let's both admit that we're guilty of jumping to conclusions." He took her hand in his big one as she met his gaze. "If I promise to stop attempting to revamp your ladybug business and your journalism career, will you try to keep your causes out of our private life and to give me the benefit of the doubt?"

Cassie smiled tremulously. "Do we have a private life?" Her voice carried a mixture of hope and humor.

Jack pulled her closer. "You bet we do," he murmured right before he kissed her.

"Watch out or I'll step on you." Cassie pushed Crystal out of the way with a gentle nudge of her toe. Even though she was in a bad mood, there was no way she'd actually hurt the cat.

The day promised to be a hot one, and the last thing she wanted to do, or had time for, was to picket the Hoffman project. Several other people had dropped out of the protest, and she didn't want to let Bonnie down, but Cassie meant to tell her that it would be her last time. She hoped that Jack wouldn't find out.

"Well, if I have to go," Cassie said to the cat who was watching her put iced tea into a thermos, "I'm darn well going to be comfortable."

Next door, Jack was helping his father take out a dogwood tree that was dying. He'd seen Cassie's car in the driveway when he got there, and he'd hoped she might be outside puttering, but so far he hadn't gotten a glimpse of her.

"Well, let's do it," his father said after Jack had circled the tree several times, glancing over his shoulder at Cassie's house. "Maybe the sound of the chain saw will rouse our young neighbor's curiosity."

Jack could feel his cheeks heating as he met his father's amused gaze. Had he been that transparent? Resisting a last look, he fired up the saw and cut off one of the eighteen-foot tree's lower limbs. The dogwood was still small enough that after they trimmed several dead branches they planned to fell the trunk onto the road, drag it aside and cut it up.

Jack had just sheared off the last limb they planned to trim when Cassie emerged from her house wearing a large sun hat and lugging a lawn chair. Jack cut the motor and walked toward the fence.

"Going to the beach?" he asked.

Cassie put the chair into the back seat of her car before replying. "No, I thought I'd get a little sun." She smiled and hurried back to the house as Jack stood watching.

When she came out again she was carrying a tote bag and a thermos. Curious, Jack walked around the end of the fence and stood by the open door of her car. Something in her expression bothered him—something furtive.

"Going alone?"

"I'm meeting some people there." She glanced in the general vicinity of his nose before turning away.

When she came back out again she was carrying some sheets of rolled up cardboard and her expression had a militant edge to it. Jack suddenly realized just where she was probably going to catch those rays.

He matched his steps to hers, speaking earnestly. "Cassie, I've heard rumors. You shouldn't go down to the job site today. It could be dangerous."

Cassie stepped around him and tossed the signs onto the back seat, slamming the door. "I promised I'd go." Her chin was thrust out.

Jack grabbed her arm as she turned back toward the house, painfully aware of his father watching the whole thing from his side of the driveway. "It's not safe," Jack insisted as she tried to shake free. "You could get hurt."

"I'll be perfectly fine, and you promised you wouldn't try to control my life." Cassie pulled loose, examining her upper arm for bruises, and headed back into the house as Jack fumed.

He followed, almost walking on the heels of her sandals. "Cassie!" he bellowed, irritated, as the screen door slammed in his face. How could one attractive, intelligent woman be so pigheaded? He yanked open the flimsy screen door and went inside.

Cassie came back through the hallway, squeezing past him. He whirled and when she went down the porch steps he was right behind her.

"Cassie, I want to talk to you!"

"Later," she said, not pausing. "I'm in a hurry."

"We need to talk now."

She stopped abruptly and he collided with her, one hand shooting out to keep her from stumbling.

"What?" Her tone was exasperated, and they were almost nose to nose.

"I know that I promised—"

"Good, that's right," she said. "You did promise, so stick to it."

Circling him, she ran lightly up the steps. He was just going in the door when she came back out, carrying a stack of flyers. "Here," she said, thrusting one into his hand. "Read this."

He glanced at the heading. Save Our Natural Environment was printed in bold letters. He thrust the paper at his father, who was leaning his elbows on the top of the fence, grinning and smoking a cigarette. "Here, you read it."

"Son, I wish your mother was home to see this," Jack's father said before he bent his attention to the sheet of paper.

"Cute," Jack snarled, totally frustrated.

Cassie had placed the pile of flyers into the car and was going back up the porch, keys in hand. "Here, kitty, kitty," she called through the open doorway. Blake and Crystal raced out before she closed and locked the door.

Jack moved and she ducked around him once again, purse in hand. "Damn it, Cassie, will you stand still," he growled as he tried to step in front of her and she dodged him. "I forbid you to risk your neck by going down there today. I told you that I heard it's going to get violent. A whole bunch of men who're out of work are planning to teach the picketers a lesson. One of my men overheard the talk at the tavern last night."

When she gave no indication of answering him, he grabbed her upper arms and hauled her close. "I don't want you to get hurt!"

She wiggled, trying to get loose, eyes wide and cheeks flushed. "Let me go. If what you said is true, I have to get down there and warn my friends," she said. "I said I'd be there. Don't you understand, I gave my word."

Jack's grip tightened. "What about me?" He was shouting again. "Don't I count? I care about you, and I care about your precious neck. *Please* don't go down there."

Sam Okimoto had called Jack the night before, cautioning him to stay well away from the job site until the picketers had been disbursed once and for all. The Yano Corporation didn't want any more publicity, and word that Jack had physically evicted Cassie had spread.

Cassie gave one last yank and freed herself as what he said registered. He cared about her, but did he care about the job more? The anger and frustration in his voice had sent the cats scurrying to safety beneath Cassie's car. Momentarily stunned by his words, Cassie almost wished she could join them. Instead she searched Jack's face for any sign of tenderness, of real affection. His eyes were blazing and his mouth had thinned above the stubborn set of his jaw.

"You'd say anything to keep me away from there, wouldn't you?" she cried, hurt at his insincerity.

Jack raked one hand through his hair, wishing for a moment that he could wrap it around her neck, instead. "I want to protect you, but I've been ordered to stay away from there. I'll screw things up with Sam if I go down there now, and I don't want to do that, but I don't want you hurt, either. Don't make me choose between you and something so important to the future of my company," he pleaded.

His hands were balled into fists and his face was a study in helpless frustration as they stared at each other.

"I'm not asking—" Before Cassie could finish, the phone in her house began to ring. She glanced from Jack's face to the locked door. "Damn," she muttered, racing up the steps with her keys in hand.

She heard Jack follow her into the house as she grabbed the phone on the fourth ring. "People who join protests are irresponsible," he was saying. "There are other ways to change things, legal ways, sensible ways—"

"Hello?" Cassie gestured for him to be quiet as she listened intently. "You're where?"

She stood with the receiver pressed to her ear, her expression unreadable as Jack circled to face her. "I see." Her voice had become curiously subdued, and Jack wondered who was on the other end of the line.

After several long moments, Cassie put her hand over the receiver. "It's my mother. She's been arrested."

His jaw dropped. "Arrested?" he repeated. "Why?"

Cassie's face colored, and she shifted her gaze to the wall behind him. "There was a demonstration at the new fur salon at the mall—"

Jack slapped an open palm against his forehead. "Of course," he crowed, "I should have known. Like mother, like daughter, right? Lunacy really does run in families." He was still seething at her total lack of reaction to his admission that he cared about her, and his temper was dangerously close to the edge of a total blowout.

Cassie was glaring, and they could both hear a tinny voice coming from the receiver. "Cassie, what's going on there?"

"That's where you'll end up next," Jack said hotly. "Perhaps you and your mother can share a cell."

"That might make things pretty crowded," Cassie drawled, a gloating light in her eyes. "She's already got a cell mate. Your mother is with her."

It was gratifying to see Jack so totally speechless for once, Cassie thought, watching the parade of expressions cross his face, even if it took such an extreme measure to bring him to this state.

"I'll be right down," she said into the phone, listening for a moment before she hung up.

"Want to go down with me and break them out?" she asked rashly, thinking that Jack deserved to sweat for a few minutes after what he'd said.

"My mother's in jail? I don't understand." He sounded as if he'd been poleaxed with a two-by-four.

After a moment, Cassie decided to take pity on him and explain what had really happened. "It's not as bad as it sounds," she said. "I'll tell you on the way."

"Dad will want to go. We can take his car." Some of the color was beginning to return to Jack's face.

On the way downtown, Cassie explained to both Jack and his father that the two women had been shopping when they'd walked into a crowd of protesters in front of Frederick's Furs. Before they realized what was happening and could work their way through the tightly packed group, a fight broke out and riot police gathered up the whole bunch, including the two perfectly innocent older women.

Things were finally sorted out at the police station, and now the mothers needed transportation back to Virginia Culpepper's car. A policeman had offered to take them, but they had decided that one ride in a squad car was enough.

"We're so glad both you and Cassie could come down," Mattie chirped to Jack as the small group left the station.

Far from being any worse for wear after their unexpected adventure, the women had managed to make it painfully obvious that they were more interested in seeing Cassie and Jack together than in retelling the story of their arrest.

"Did we interrupt some plans you young people had?" Cassie's mother asked from the back seat as they drove away.

"You might say that," Jack replied grimly, snapping his seat belt with a loud click. "Cassie was on her way to the picket line to protest my latest and most-important building project, and I was trying to stop her from possibly getting her head bashed in."

"And not very effectively," his father added.

"By your men, dear?" his mother asked.

Jack, who was driving, glared into the rearview mirror. "No, mother, not by my people. Most likely by her own."

"And why is that, dear?" his mother asked.

Jack just shook his head. "Trying to stop Cassie is like trying to stop a runaway freight train," he complained to his father who was sitting beside him in the front seat. "Was Mom ever that stubborn?"

"Oh, she let me chase her until she caught me," Fred Hoffman replied, making the two older women giggle.

Sandwiched between the two ladies in the back seat, Cassie could feel the color splash across her cheeks. Did everyone have to discuss her as if she wasn't even there?

After they dropped Cassie's mother at the mall to pick up her car, the four others drove back home. Thanking Fred Hoffman for driving, Cassie got out and walked over to her Volkswagen.

"You're not still going?" Jack asked as he came up beside her.

"Of course. I already told you I was, and I'm late." All she really intended to do was to warn the others about the rumors of violence Jack had heard. She took a deep breath after she'd gotten in the car. "I really wish you'd just stay out of my life," she said, turning the key.

"Fine." Jack bristled with suppressed violence. "I'll do just that."

"Fine," she said, putting the car into reverse.

"Fine," he repeated, stepping away from the car.

She backed down the driveway, trying her best to ignore the sight of his imposing figure glaring after her, feet widespread and arms folded against his broad chest. "Fine," she muttered to herself. So much for their resolutions to keep their private lives separate. Jack couldn't keep from trying to control her, even for a couple of days.

Cassie ended up doing her share of picket duty as the ground breaking was delayed and the local newspaper devoted several columns to the pros and cons of the whole issue. Dispirited over her last argument with Jack, she saw no point in quitting the protest.

No one from the Yano Corporation or from Hoffman Construction came to the site, but she read an extensive interview by Sam Okimoto along with one by the protest leader.

Cassie had to admit that, side by side, the argument for jobs and new development came across as sounding more important than saving the nesting area of some common waterfowl and small animals. The opposition's stand was further strengthened by a professor from Sacramento who pointed out that there were several undeveloped acres of wetlands only miles from the controversial site. Cassie hadn't realized that.

The protesters could tell that the tide was turning against them by the shrinking of their numbers during the next few days, which was another reason Cassie hadn't said anything about quitting.

Tempers were running high between Cassie's group and the other faction on one particularly hot afternoon. There had been a persistent rumor that something was going to happen then; that and the heat had combined to make everyone especially tense.

Channel 3 had promised to send a news team, and Cassie's group was determined to mount one last effort although the cause was starting to look hopeless. Cassie herself longed for the whole thing to be over; the doubts that had been raised in her mind about the real importance of stopping the project refused to be squelched, and she wanted to find out if there was anything left to save of her budding relationship with Jack.

She missed him with a raw ache that would not be appeased. Tom had finally come for dinner and had talked about Jack until she asked him to drop the subject. Tom's dawning comprehension had done nothing for her pride or her bruised heart, but he had quickly changed the subject to a party their parents were planning.

"Better not go alone," Tom advised darkly. "If you do, mother will spend the evening introducing you to eligible males."

"I don't want to meet any males, eligible or otherwise," Cassie had replied pettishly. His warning depressed her even further. She didn't want a man, except for Jack, and she wasn't ready to meet anyone new.

Now she wiped a damp hand across her perspiring brow as she shifted the sign that had grown steadily heavier and turned to an equally wilted woman who'd been marching alongside her all afternoon.

"I don't like the way that one group of men is getting louder and more belligerent," Cassie said under her breath. "They've been drinking beer for hours, and they really look ugly."

"Honey, those men looked ugly when they were born," her companion drawled. "I just wish the television people would get here to film their footage so we could all go home." She took a swig of warm lemonade and walked away, carrying her tattered sign at half-mast. To Cassie the woman's drooping shoulders said she'd already admitted defeat.

Two things began to happen simultaneously. The men who'd been drinking beer and shouting insults began to advance on Cassie's group holding their bottles like clubs, and Jack's truck bounced into the rutted driveway raising a choking cloud of dust. Right behind him was the van from Channel 3.

The hair on the back of Cassie's neck stood up when her attention returned to the expressions on the faces of the advancing men. They obviously drew courage from each other and had managed to whip themselves into a frenzy of violence. Cassie began to retreat, but it was too late. She was caught in the human tide of bodies.

Jack and another man leaped from the truck. Cassie noticed they were wearing hard hats and carrying baseball bats. For a moment she was distracted by the authority that surrounded Jack like a cloak, and she prayed he wouldn't get hurt. Then she concentrated once again on her own safety. Things were happening too fast.

"I don't think we're going to have any luck with that low profile you were hoping for," John Clearwater muttered to Jack as boos and catcalls went up around them. "They've noticed us."

Jack was too busy searching the crowd for Cassie to reply, almost too preoccupied to hear the wail of distant sirens. Several skirmishes had broken out among the younger men, but the majority of the picketers were retreating from the middle of the area. Many older men and women were heading quickly toward their cars as the team from Channel 3 tried to interview anyone who cared to comment.

"You shouldn't be here," John said from Jack's right as they pushed farther into the milling throng. "Sam made it very clear that he wanted you away from the limelight. His people are pressuring him, too, you know. No more publicity."

"I have to find Cassie." Damn, where had all these people come from? Even with the ones who were leaving, there must be a hundred left. He raised one arm absently, a lump of worry blocking his throat, as a woman batted at him with her cardboard sign.

"Pirate!" she cried. "Robber baron!"

Jack would have smiled if he hadn't been so desperate to find one medium-sized brunette with pansy-brown eyes and a razor-sharp tongue.

Then the crowd shifted, and he got a glimpse of Cassie's dark hair and red shirt. Trust her to be smack in the middle of the action, surrounded by the rough-looking bunch he'd noticed there before, the ones who looked like escapees from a motorcycle movie.

Jack pushed harder, aware of John protecting his back as he struggled to get to Cassie.

"Jack! Jack Hoffman!"

He turned at the sound of his name. The reporter from Channel 3 was trying to catch up to him, her cameraman trailing behind.

Jack shook his head at her repeated gestures to wait. "Not now," he shouted. Not ever, he thought silently. Sam would have him shanghaied if he was on television. No, not shanghaied, he thought on a note of sour humor, wrong ethnic group. Sealed into the trunk of a Japanese subcompact car.

Cassie had almost forgotten her surprise at seeing Jack there, knowing what his presence could cost him, when the big hulk who seemed to be the ringleader of the violent faction addressed her directly. He was the same man who'd been encouraging everyone to "mix it up" all afternoon and had been passing out beer from a huge cooler in the back of his disreputable van.

"You should be home tending your babies and fixing your old man's dinner," he bawled into her face.

Cassie fanned away his beery breath with her hand and thrust out her chin. She didn't care how big he was, there was no way she was going to back away from his macho challenge.

"I don't have any babies, and I'm not some man's household help," she shouted back at him. "Why aren't you out looking for work instead of trying to start World War III down here?"

Several women behind her cheered.

The man scowled, his little bloodshot eyes glaring murderously. Apparently he hadn't expected her to answer him.

"You better go home and make some babies, then," he said, his insolent smirk revealing rotten teeth. "Maybe I better go home with you and help." He flung a hairy arm around her shoulders as the men around him applauded and egged him on.

"Get your filthy paws off me!" Cassie shouted, trying not to breathe in his odor of stale beer and even staler sweat.

"You heard her!" A voice like thunder commanded behind them. "Take your hands off her."

Cassie almost sagged with relief at the sound of Jack's voice. She glanced up into his murderous face, thinking that she'd never been so happy to see anyone.

"Find your own breeder," the man drawled. "This one's mine."

"*Breeder!* Why you—" she began to sputter.

"Shut up, Cass." Jack's voice had turned ice-cold as he handed his bat to the man behind him.

Wisely, Cassie decided it wasn't time to protest either Jack's bossiness or the scumball's degrading description.

Her gaze snapped from one bristling male to the other. The stranger must be half-drunk not to realize the danger he was in. Jack's hard face beneath the silver helmet radiated violence, and his muscles stood out in sharp relief as he waited with arms braced, big hands clenched into fists. Behind him his companion watched the crowd, protecting Jack's back with the bats he gripped in his brown hands.

The man who had accosted Cassie finally slid his arm away from her as the surrounding crush of spectators stepped back, forming a rough circle. Cassie shrugged as if that would rid her of his offensive touch. She glared but he and Jack were eyeing each other like wolves wanting to lead the same pack. Behind Jack the black-haired man spoke.

"Remember Sam Okimoto, boss," he said nervously. "Let's grab your girl and get out of here before that cameraman catches up with us."

Cassie looked at Jack, wondering if he'd heard the warning. His attention was focused entirely on the scruffy man who'd called Cassie a breeder. At that point she didn't care about the insult; she only wanted Jack out of there. She moved forward, thinking that if she went with him they could leave before he got into trouble.

As Cassie walked between the two men, the greasy-looking tormenter gave her a shove, almost sending her to her knees. "Yer stayin' with me," he sneered. "Ya can take this guy on next if ya want, but I getcha first."

"Start filming!" shouted a female voice, seconds before Jack's fist shot out and connected with the other man's whiskery chin. The man went down in a heap as fists started flying in every direction. Jack grabbed Cassie's hand and pulled her along as his companion followed behind, wielding his bat.

"Nice move, boss," John Clearwater said as they got to the truck. "We come down here after you promised me you'd keep out of trouble, and instead you start a brawl. You'd better start thinking about how you're going to explain all this to Sam."

Chapter Ten

Cassie and Tom sat glumly in front of her television, the uneaten portions of their stir-fried vegetables growing cold on their plates. Ever since Jack and his friend John had dropped her at the house, she'd been wallowing in guilt, confusion and depression.

"Are you sure that the reporter was there when Jack hit the other guy?" Tom asked her for the third time. "Maybe they missed that part."

Cassie shook her head and pushed at the congealing dinner with her fork. "When I looked around, the reporter had the most ecstatic expression on her face, like she'd walked in on a major drug bust. I'm just sure she caught the action, and I don't know what it will mean to Jack's future if the rep from that Japanese company finds out he was down there."

The Kitty Kibbles commercial finally ended, and the opening credits of the evening news began to roll.

"If only—" Cassie began to moan, fists clenched tightly.

"Shhh," Tom interrupted. "The announcer's talking about the protest."

"Violence broke out today at the Yano Corporation construction site, scene of recent environmental controversy," the announcer droned as the screen jumped to a picture of the picketers. "The man wearing the hard hat has been identified as Jack Hoffman, owner of the construction company that is going to build the industrial park that has been the center of the ongoing dispute."

Cassie groaned and leaned closer to the television. Jack looked disturbingly masculine, his expression righteous and the muscles of his arms bulging as he coiled his considerable strength and released the punch that flattened Cassie's tormentor.

"Oh, damn," she muttered.

"Mr. Hoffman wasn't available for comment," the announcer continued, "but we did manage to interview several of the demonstrators from both sides of the issue. Before we run that tape, let me say that riot police were able to break things up and send everyone home before anyone other than a Mr. Pigsticker Black, who suffered from a badly swollen jaw, was injured."

Cassie leaped up and pushed the Off button. "Oh, why did he do that?" she wailed. "His friend *told* him they weren't supposed to be there. I wonder if Jack could lose the whole contract over this."

Her brother rose, too, and put a comforting arm around her shoulders. "If you don't know why he did it, you're a lot slower than I am," he drawled. "And I doubt they could fire Jack at this late date. They were already scheduled to break ground before your friends decided to meddle."

Cassie pulled away and picked up their dishes. "It seemed like a good idea at the time," she mumbled.

"It's not like you to leap into something like this without getting all the facts," he continued, picking up their glasses and following her to the kitchen. "What gives?"

Cassie thought a moment while she scraped the remains of their dinners into the garbage. "I guess my mind was elsewhere," she said slowly. "Or maybe I just wanted a cause to support." She remembered how steamed she'd been at Jack, how ready to take a stand against almost any threat to the environment, and how she'd leaped when Bonnie had called. What a mess.

Beside her, Tom began running water into the sink. "You could call him," he suggested.

"Oh, no, I couldn't do that. He was furious when he left, and I'm sure he's fed up with rescuing me."

"And how do you feel?" Sometimes her brother's persistence grated on Cassie's nerves.

"I wish we could start over," she confessed, wiping the tile countertop. "I really, I really—" Tears spilled over and began to dribble down her cheeks as she hastily excused herself and rushed to the bedroom, shutting the door behind her.

After Cassie had calmed down and wiped at her face with a cool cloth, regretting her outburst, she lay on her bed for a few more moments before going back to the kitchen.

Images of Jack's smiling face taunted her, memories of his sweet, sizzling kisses made her roll over and grab her pillow with both fists. He'd tried to show her that they could have a relationship, but she hadn't had enough faith in them, and now it was too late. She'd loved and lost, she thought dramatically, and she'd have to learn to get along without the white knight who'd sacrificed so much to save her thick, stubborn hide.

With a last sigh and a swipe at her nose, Cassie got up and rejoined Tom.

"Are you okay?" he asked, putting away the last dry dish.

Cassie glanced around. He'd cleaned up everything and washed the dishes. The kitchen was immaculate. There was a lot to be said for bachelor brothers.

"Yes." She sighed. "I'll be all right."

"I still think you should call him," Tom urged. "If he cared enough to rescue you..." His voice trailed off as Cassie shook her head violently.

"That's just his nature," she insisted. "Rescuing people has nothing to do with any deep, abiding affection for me. It's just something that Jack can't help doing." She thought of Herb Applebaum and Jack's own mother. "It's something he can't help," she repeated, almost to herself.

While Cassie was telling Tom goodbye on her front porch, Jack was having a conference with Sam Okimoto. Jack had wasted no time after he'd dropped Cassie at her house, a plan already forming in his head. After some hasty checking to make sure his idea was feasible, he had returned John Clearwater to his car and thanked him for the support.

"Good luck with your idea," John said sincerely. "It could be just the ticket to win your fair damsel."

"I want to do it because it's the right thing," Jack insisted hotly. "It has nothing to do with that brainless little firebrand. Imagine her taking on that big bozo. It still makes my gut twist to think of his greasy hands on her."

"Yeah," John drawled, nodding. "What you're trying to pull off has nothing to do with Cassie." He laughed and tossed off a wave. "Good luck, whatever your motives are. See you tomorrow."

"If we still have a contract," Jack answered, pulling away.

Some time later, Jack was knocking on Sam Okimoto's hotel room door, file folder in hand. He sent up a short prayer that Sam would be in a receptive mood.

"Ah," the older man said as he opened the door and saw who was there. "If it isn't the star of the five o'clock news."

Two mornings later, Jack walked the deserted building site once again. This time he paid close attention to the marshy section toward the back of the property and the little stream that meandered through the woodsy area behind the back boundary. Before, he'd looked at that section as a problem that had to be solved, but now he studied it with new eyes, aware of the birds that flew into the sky at his approach and the faint, rustling noises he could hear in the tall grass all around him.

A feeling of peace, the first calm moments he'd had in days, stole over him as he sat on a partially rotted log and stuck the tender tip of a long weed stalk between his teeth. Actually, it had been weeks, not days since he'd been himself, he amended. Ever since Cassie had decided he needed a cold shower, his life had been turned topsy-turvy.

As Jack finally rose with a sigh and headed back to his truck, he couldn't help but hope that Sam would have good news when he called, for Cassie, for himself, and for all the little creatures he could hear scuttling out of the way as his heavy work boots carried him back through the tall grasses.

The same morning, Cassie was working feverishly to process the new loads of ladybugs she'd completely forgotten were coming in that day. She hadn't printed out any invoices or mailing labels yet, and orders were stacked on her desk and all over the table in the garage. She was tired from staying up late the night before to finish her column before her deadline, and irritable from lack of sleep. Even the cats knew well enough to stay out of her way.

When the telephone rang at noon she snarled a greeting, realized how hostile she sounded and began again.

"Hello," she repeated, clearing her throat as if the first growl had merely been a misplaced frog.

"Hello yourself, sweetheart. Catching a cold?"

The sound of Jack's deep, husky voice coming through the line made her drop the receiver in surprise. He was the last person she had expected to hear from. Ever. And he'd called her sweetheart.

"Jack?" she questioned cautiously as she picked up the receiver after it had thudded against the wall three times.

"Yes, honey, it's me. Please don't drop the phone again."

Cassie was glad he wasn't there to see her blush. Her fingers tightened their grip. "Why are you calling?" What did they have to say to each other after the last fiasco?

"Sam Okimoto is having a press conference at his hotel this afternoon, and I'd like you to be there," Jack said. "I think you'll find what he has to say pretty interesting. At least I hope so."

"You didn't get fired?"

Jack thought of the first few blistering moments in Sam's hotel room two evenings before and winced at the memory. Sam had used his tongue like a samurai sword until Jack had finally managed to divert him.

"No, I didn't get fired. And, no, I'm not going to tell you anything else. The press conference is at the Hyatt House at 3:00 p.m. See you there."

Before Cassie could say anything else there was a loud click signaling that Jack had hung up. Stunned, she stared at the phone. Trust him to raise her curiosity and then leave her to be eaten up by it. Damn the man! She glanced at the clock and then back at the bags of ladybugs. She'd have to hurry if she expected to be ready on time.

Jack searched the room anxiously, looking for Cassie's dark head in the crowd of media types. It seemed he was always searching through unruly throngs looking for her, and he suspected he would be doing the same thing again sometime or other, unless she changed quite a bit.

Beside him at the table, Sam shuffled papers and turned to look at the draped board behind them.

"Any sign of her?" Sam asked, understanding in his voice.

Jack shook his head, then he spotted Cassie at the back of the conference room. "There she is!"

"If you'd rather be with her than up here with me, I would understand," Sam said, a slight smile pulling at his thin lips.

"Uh—" Jack glanced at the other man, then back at Cassie, who looked ready to bolt at any second. "Thanks," he said over his shoulder as he rose and hurried across the room.

Behind him, Sam Okimoto, who'd been educated in the United States and had married a Japanese-American career woman with a mind of her own, smiled wider and shook his head. Jack would have his hands full, but Sam knew from experience that he would enjoy every moment of it, as Sam himself had done.

Cassie saw Jack coming toward her and experienced the flush of pleasure she always did when looking at his handsome face and imposing figure, dressed formally this afternoon in a lightweight powder-blue suit and silk tie. She was glad that she had taken the time to put on a coral-and-white print skirt and cotton sweater before coming. The flattering outfit gave her a shot of false courage as Jack worked his way determinedly through the crowd of reporters, many of them from Sacramento.

Jack's expression was serious, reminding her of all that lay between them, and she twisted her hands together wishing again that she hadn't come. Seeing him once more, perhaps for the last time, would be a cruel experience. She hadn't thought that Jack was the kind of man who would parade his victory before her with unfeeling exultation, but a tiny doubt had been niggling at her since his phone call, growing larger as she drove to the hotel and parked, then found her way to the room where the press conference was being held.

Before she could turn and retreat, Jack was beside her.

"Hi," he said, his eyes blazing down at her as he shoved his hands into his pockets. "Glad you could make it."

Cassie searched his face for any clues to the nature of the announcement Sam Okimoto was going to make. Although Jack radiated suppressed excitement, she couldn't tell how to interpret his expression.

At the front of the room, Sam Okimoto had risen and was asking the crowd for silence. Jack took Cassie's hand and tucked it into the crook of his elbow, then turned to listen.

"As you all know," Sam was saying into the bank of microphones, "the building of our new plant here in Palmerton has not been without controversy. We at Yano want to be good neighbors, as we have always been in other communities in the past." He cleared his throat and went on as flashbulbs popped.

"It was far into the planning stages of our new electronics complex that a contingent of citizens began to object to our location because of a certain section of boggy ground we had included in our development. Contrary to popular belief, we did search, diligently I might add, for another piece of property that would suit our particular needs."

Cassie tried to pull her hand away from Jack's arm as she stood with her chin thrust forward, sickeningly afraid now that he really had brought her here to listen to the announcement that building would begin immediately.

He caught her retreating hand with his, holding it firm. "Be patient, little firebug," he whispered. "And don't jump to conclusions."

Their eyes met in a long stare as Sam's voice droned on. Something deep in Jack's eyes, a pure light that glowed brighter and brighter, connected with an answering spark of hope that started in Cassie's heart and began to radiate outward.

Before them, Sam had stepped over to the draped board. "It was too late to alter our plans without great expense," he continued, pulling the cloth away from a colorful map. "But, thanks to the research and timely suggestion of the general contractor of our complex, Jack Hoffman, we have found what we hope is a suitable solution."

He turned back to the microphones. "Yano Corporation has bought ten acres of wetlands along Drury Creek adjoining our building site, and we have set aside funds and taken steps to guarantee that this property will be left in its natural state, to be forever held in trust for the animals and birds displaced by our new plant."

There was a stunned silence, then the room erupted into a cacophony of reporters' aggressive questions. Cassie stood in shock, scarcely able to believe what she had heard. Wordless, she turned questioning eyes to Jack.

"You did this?" she whispered as he grinned down at her.

With the way she was looking at him, it was all Jack could do not to kiss her right there. "No," he corrected patiently, "I only suggested it. Sam thought it was a hell of an idea, and he's the one who got the wheels turning and presented the idea to his superiors. The land was purchased this morning, and I got the word from Sam right before I called you."

Jack held his breath as he waited for Cassie to say something, anything. Before she did, Sam Okimoto spoke Jack's name through a mike up front. When Jack turned impatiently, Sam was motioning him to come forward.

"Wait here," he told Cassie. "I'll be back as soon as I can."

She watched his broad shoulders as he worked his way through the crowd, pride and happiness bringing tears to her eyes. He'd changed so much since they had first met. He clasped Sam's outstretched hand, then shook hands with Palmerton's mayor before answering questions from the floor.

As Cassie tried to assimilate all she had just learned, a new thought entered her head. Just because Jack had changed his viewpoint didn't necessarily mean he'd done it for love of her. All their arguments, all their disagreements—didn't they stem from a basic incompatibility? Surely their love, if he did love her, would have helped them to understand and to compromise.

The thought that it might be too late for them, even as everything else was at long last working out, was an overwhelming one. Cassie continued to watch Jack as the doubts began to mushroom. What she needed was time to think, to sort through everything that had been said and done, and she needed to do it alone. Her own love wasn't in doubt; it was stronger than ever after what he'd brought about. It was Jack's intentions she couldn't bear to dissect in such a public place.

With a last glance at his shining head and the devastating image he presented in the well-tailored suit, Cassie turned and began to make her way to the door at the rear of the room.

The instant she moved toward the exit, Jack was aware of her imminent departure. A reporter from the *Sacramento Bee* had been asking him something about his company, but Jack missed the question, wondering instead if Cassie was leaving because he'd done what she wanted and she had no further use for him.

"Excuse me," he said to the startled reporter. "There's something I have to take care of right away."

When he came out the front door of the hotel, he spotted Cassie getting into her car. Thankful that he'd parked directly across the street, Jack sprinted down the steps as she drove away.

Cassie was totally oblivious to the traffic around her, intent only on getting to the small park behind the office complex a mile down the road. Tears filled her eyes, and pain made her hands tremble on the wheel as she signaled for the turn and drove through the parking lot to the small, private area of grass and rosebushes beyond. The sprinklers were turned on in half of the park, but the wrought-iron bench beneath a majestic weeping willow where she'd come on other occasions was dry and deserted.

Jack saw her turn in ahead of him. He followed at a distance as she parked and got out, unaware of his approaching truck. Her head was bent and her shoulders drooped as if she'd gotten bad news instead of good. What could be bothering her? he wondered as he pulled into an empty spot.

In a way he was glad she'd left the busy meeting. Privacy suited him, but her actions were still puzzling. Anyone glimpsing her dejected posture would assume she had just lost her best friend.

If Cassie thought she had seen the last of him now that she'd gotten what she wanted, she had better think again, he decided with a determined smile. Stripping off his jacket and tie in deference to the hot day, Jack tossed them on the seat and rolled up his sleeves before walking to the bench where Cassie sat huddled with her back to him.

She had stopped crying and was giving herself a pep talk when he walked noiselessly up behind her. "I won't give up," she said out loud. "No two people could go through what we have without caring deeply for each other. It's *not* over."

"I'm glad to hear that, as long as it's me you're talking about," Jack said from directly behind her. His voice startled Cassie so badly that she jumped up, shrieking.

Before she could say anything, Jack had circled the bench and reached out his arms. "Come here," he said. "You're right, it's far from over."

Cassie could scarcely believe he was standing before her. With a glad cry, she launched herself into his embrace, wrapping her arms around his neck. Jack folded her to him, picking her right off the ground and swinging her in a circle before he set her carefully on her feet again.

His eyes glowed with an intense light from within, and the smile beneath his thick mustache was so wide it carved deep lines into his cheeks. Cassie touched his lone dimple with her finger, and he caught her hand in his and brought it to his mouth.

"I have something to discuss with you," Jack said, a slight tremor in his voice. He laced his fingers with hers and pulled her back down to the bench with him, shifting his body so that he was facing her. His complexion was flushed beneath his tan, and his breathing was agitated, making Cassie's own pulses race in response.

"I love you," Jack said after a moment of silence, his voice a gravelly purr as his eyes burned into hers. "Despite every obstacle nature has thrown between us, I've come to love you very much, and to admire your courage and your sense of honor." He stopped and dropped a kiss onto the back of the hand he still gripped tightly. "And I want you so much that it's driving me crazy." His voice lowered to a more intimate tone. "If you knew the nights I've lain awake thinking of you, you'd take pity on me and say something," he continued, only half joking. "Tell me how you feel. I don't want to go on any longer without you."

New tears filled Cassie's eyes, and she dashed them away with her free hand. "I love you, too," she murmured, smiling at the breath he let out at her words. She rested her palm against his cheek, happier than she'd ever been. "I never thought we'd get this far."

"I did," he said, some of his natural arrogance returning. "I knew somehow we'd make it."

"Are we having another argument?" Cassie teased
lightly, happiness filling her so completely she thought
she'd rise from the bench like a hot-air balloon.

"No, ma'am," Jack rasped. "Though I'm sure we will
have our share of arguments in the future. Let's just
make a promise to always end them like this." He lowered his head, his lips covering hers in a searing kiss that
sent shock waves through her body. Cassie's arms tightened around his neck as her lips parted beneath the
warmth of his mouth, taking him in and caressing his
tongue with her own.

After a long, blissful moment, he lifted his head and
sighed tenderly, resting his chin against her hair.

"You feel so good in my arms," he murmured, "but
now I have an important question to ask."

Cassie was still overwhelmed by the joy of hearing that
he loved her and the heady seduction of his kiss.

"Question?"

He stood and reached into his pant pocket, pulling out
a small, flat box. Cassie's heart fluttered for a moment,
but she knew it wasn't the right shape to hold a ring.
Marriage didn't necessarily follow love these days, even
though she was certain that marriage was what she
wanted to share with Jack. Still, they had plenty of time
for him to realize that their love was going to last a life-
time, she reminded herself.

He'd opened the lid and Cassie glanced down at the
gold-and-diamond pendant winking in the sunlight.

"I got this weeks ago," Jack said, drawing her attention back to his face, "and then things got complicated
and I never gave it to you. I hope that you'll accept it now
as a sign of my love."

Cassie tore her gaze away from the expression of devotion on his face and looked closer. Nestled on blue velvet was a small gold ladybug set with diamonds, strung on a delicate chain.

"It's perfect," she gasped.

"It's you. I couldn't resist it."

When he'd fastened it around her neck and she touched it carefully with her fingertips, Jack cleared his throat nervously and interrupted when she tried to thank him.

"I thought you would like to pick out a ring together," he said in a rush, "but I hope that from this moment on you'll consider us engaged. That is, if you'll agree to marry me." The color had again flushed his face except for white strain lines around his mouth.

As Cassie remained speechless, he hurried on. "I know we can make a go of it. Deep down we're not so different, and I'm proud of what you do. I won't stand in your way if there's a cause you want to support...I'd even help if I could."

His smile was ragged around the edges as he continued, "I won't give you any unwanted advice. You can run things exactly as you have been." He paused and swallowed as Cassie's heart filled with happiness.

"Cassie," he continued on a note of desperation, "I want us to share our lives. I promise you can check over every blueprint, every job bid I get if you like, but give us a chance, okay?"

Cassie could wait no longer to give him her answer. She threw her arms around his neck, joy cascading over her. "Yes!" she cried, disturbing a nearby bird. "Oh, yes, Jack. I will marry you! I know we'll be the happiest couple in three counties."

"Six," he said smugly.

For a timeless moment they held each other tightly as Cassie did her best to absorb all that had just happened. Jack's hands made long, sweeping caresses down her back, and her own fingers were entwined in the hair at his nape. When he lifted his face, she met his mouth eagerly in a kiss that was both promise and tribute.

He released her slowly, his breathing shallow and rapid. "There's one thing we didn't consider," he said gravely.

Cassie stiffened. Second thoughts already? She held her breath as a teasing smile crinkled the corners of his eyes. "Do you realize how much flak we're going to get from our mothers? You know they'll think of a way to take full credit for our engagement."

Cassie's laugh was a joyous sound. "It will probably take the pressure off my brother for a while. Mother will be so busy with wedding plans." She paused, worried. "Do you mind a big wedding?" she asked timidly. "It's something Mother has had her heart set on since I was small."

"And how do you feel about it?" His thick brows were raised in query.

"Since it's the only wedding I'll ever have, I would like a formal ceremony."

His smile grew wider. "I agree, and I promise it will be perfect. Karen and Ben eloped, and Mom has been itching for a real wedding. Perhaps she and your mother can work on it together."

Cassie gripped his forearm excitedly. "That would be great. We'll turn them loose to plan a wedding neither family will ever forget, and then they'll be too busy to gloat."

"There's one other thing," Jack said, rising and scooping her into his arms. "It's something I've had in mind to do since the very first time we met."

He strode purposely across the velvety lawn as Cassie, guessing his intent, began to struggle. "You wouldn't!" she laughed as he walked faster.

"Oh, yes I would. You've promised to become my wife and you can't back out now. You're wearing my bug." With a diabolical laugh he walked straight into the row of sprinklers.

Cassie shrieked as the icy water hit her.

"Enjoy it," Jack crowed above the sound of her protests as they both became soaked. "Your first engagement shower." Standing in the very middle of the sprinklers' spray, he gazed down at her, water dripping off his chin.

Cassie's laughter stopped abruptly as she returned his look of adoration.

"I do love you," he said solemnly. And he kissed her.

*   *   *   *   *

SET SAIL FOR THE SOUTH SEAS
with
BESTSELLING AUTHOR
EMILIE RICHARDS

This month Silhouette Intimate Moments begins a very special miniseries by a very special author. *Tales of the Pacific*, by Emilie Richards, will take you to Hawaii, New Zealand and Australia and introduce you to a group of men and women you will never forget.

In Book One, FROM GLOWING EMBERS, share laughter and tears with Julianna Mason and Gray Sheridan as they overcome the pain of the past and rekindle the love that had brought them together in marriage ten years ago and now, amidst the destructive force of a tropical storm, drives them once more into an embrace without end.

FROM GLOWING EMBERS (Intimate Moments #249) is available now. And in coming months look for the rest of the series: SMOKESCREEN (November 1988), RAINBOW FIRE (February 1989) and OUT OF THE ASHES (May 1989). They're all coming your way—only in Silhouette Intimate Moments.

IM249-R

Silhouette Romance

COMING NEXT MONTH

#598 VALLEY OF RAINBOWS—Rita Rainville
Liann Murphy respected the mysteries of Hawaii's past while Cody Hunter
understood the promises of its future. Could they build their dream
together in the magical valley of rainbows?

#599 SIMPLY SAM—Deana Brauer
For years Jake Silvercloud had known Samantha Smith as "tagalong"
tomboy Sam, but she'd grown up—with a vengeance—and Sam was ready
to lead the handsome rancher on a merry, loving chase....

#600 TAKING SAVANAH—Pepper Adams
Her former husband, Beau, had knocked Southern belle Savanah Winslow
off her feet with the news that they were still married. Could she resist
giving the brash Yankee another chance?

#601 THE BLAKEMORE TOUCH—Diana Reep
As his public relations consultant, Christina Hayward had to preserve
Marc Blakemore's glittering image—and maintain a professional distance.
But Marc's masterful touch was getting a firm grip on her heart....

#602 HOME AGAIN—Glenda Sands
Nicki Fox's high-school crush on Kenneth Blackwell had meant nothing—
until she went back home and found herself working with him. Now old
feelings were becoming a very adult chemistry....

#603 ANY SUNDAY—Debbie Macomber
Marjorie Majors was never squeamish—unless she got ill. Dr. Sam Bretton
had allayed her fears with his charming bedside manner, and now
Marjorie needed his *loving* care...forever.

AVAILABLE THIS MONTH:

**#592 JUSTIN—Book 2 of the
LONG, TALL TEXANS trilogy**
Diana Palmer

#593 SHERLOCK'S HOME
Sharon De Vita

#594 FINISHING TOUCH
Jane Bierce

#595 THE LADYBUG LADY
Pamela Toth

#596 A NIGHT OF PASSION
Lucy Gordon

**#597 THE KISS OF A
STRANGER**
Brittany Young

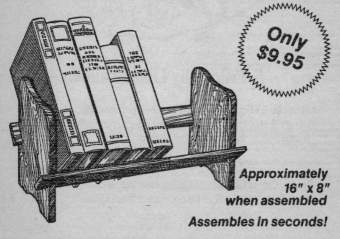

Silhouette Romance

LONG, TALL TEXANS

A Trilogy by Diana Palmer

Bestselling Diana Palmer has rustled up three rugged heroes in a trilogy sure to lasso your heart! The titles of the books are your introduction to these unforgettable men:

CALHOUN

In June, meet Calhoun Ballenger. He wants to protect Abby Clark from the world, but can he protect her from himself?

JUSTIN

Calhoun's brother, Justin—the strong, silent type—has a second chance with the woman of his dreams, Shelby Jacobs, in August.

TYLER

October's long, tall Texan is Shelby's virile brother, Tyler, who teaches shy Nell Regan to trust her instincts—especially when they lead her into his arms!

Don't miss CALHOUN, JUSTIN and TYLER—three gripping new stories coming soon from Silhouette Romance!

SRLTT